KU-168-109

LIBRARIES N
ROM STOCK

IMPETUOUS NURSE

Nurse Lynn Avery has a reputation for being a practical joker, which she uses to conceal her unhappiness after her recent break-up. But she cannot remain in the wilderness; and although Doctor Vince Braddock professes his love for her, it is Doctor Paul Morgan who has her under his spell. When Lynn accepts that she is in love, her problems are only starting, as shadows creep back into her life. Then Paul begins to show an interest in Della Tate, and matters go from bad to worse . . .

PHYLLIS MALLETT

IMPETUOUS NURSE

Complete and Unabridged

LINFORD
Leicester

First published in Great Britain in 1978

First Linford Edition
published 2017

Copyright © 1978 by Alison Bray
All rights reserved

A catalogue record for this book is available
from the British Library.

ISBN 978–1–4448–3473–4

Published by
F. A. Thorpe (Publishing)
Anstey, Leicestershire

Set by Words & Graphics Ltd.
Anstey, Leicestershire
Printed and bound in Great Britain by
T. J. International Ltd., Padstow, Cornwall

This book is printed on acid-free paper

1

Lynn Avery narrowed her blue eyes as she entered the big general hospital in the city of Stokeford on the first bright sunlit day of April. With so much rain during the past weeks she had begun to think that taking her holiday next week would be yet another big mistake of her life, but upon arising this morning she found that the rain clouds had gone and warm sunlight shone from a beautiful sky.

Although she had not planned to go away this year, she hoped to get out into the open air after the long winter months wearily walking the hospital wards. But there was no joy in her for she could recall only too well the tentative plans she and Robert had made the previous September for this very holiday. It was to have been their honeymoon.

But all that was gone, thanks to Nurse Wrenn, who had worked in Men's Surgical and been afflicted with a roving eye and no conscience when it came to love. Robert had departed from the hospital, with Nurse Wrenn, and Lynn had endured several weeks of sympathy from the rest of the staff.

There were two nurses standing in the corridor by the Sister's office of Women's Medical. One was a student nurse, the other her best friend, Chrissie Wright.

'Hello, Lynn!' Chrissie was a plump girl with brown eyes and a heart of gold. From the very first day of their training, she and Lynn had been firm friends. 'Isn't it a beautiful day out there? You're lucky, going on holiday next week. I wish I'd been free. We could have gone away together.'

'I'll probably just help Mother tidy the garden,' said Lynn in practical tones.

'That's no way to spend a holiday,' protested Chrissie.

'It's not the way I planned to spend it when I asked for next week,' countered Lynn, smiling ruefully. 'What are you waiting for? Aren't you taking over from the night staff?'

'Sister Sloan hasn't arrived yet. She's in Assistant Matron's office. You haven't been getting into trouble, have you, Lynn?'

'Trouble?' echoed Lynn. 'I never get into trouble.'

'You must be joking,' Chrissie said. 'But I will say this, I'm quite sure it's never your fault.'

'I do my duty, and as long as I know that, then nothing else matters.' Lynn turned when she heard footsteps along the corridor, and saw the short figure of Sister Sloan approaching.

'Come along then, don't stand around in the corridors, you chattering magpies,' called their superior. 'Into the ward and relieve the night staff. Just because I'm late, it doesn't mean everyone has to be late. Not you, Nurse Avery, please,' she added as Lynn began

3

to follow Chrissie and the student nurse. 'Go into the office. I want to have a word with you.'

Chrissie threw Lynn an anxious glance, but Lynn shrugged and entered the office, turning to face Sister Sloan as she breezed through the doorway.

'Has someone been using my name in vain again, Sister?' asked Lynn, referring to the past months when she had been accused of some practical joking that had broken out among the nursing staff.

'Have you developed a guilt complex?' replied her superior, her shrewd brown eyes glinting as she regarded Lynn.

'Anything is possible, but I seem to take the blame for everything that happens around here.'

Sister Sloan walked around the desk and sat down.

'No, there's nothing wrong that I know of. But I have been talking to Assistant Matron, and I'm afraid I have to ask you to consider postponing your holiday for the time being. Nurse Atkinson has reported that her young daughter has gone down with German measles, and Nurse Atkinson hasn't had it so she will be off duty for three weeks.'

'That's all right, Sister. I haven't made any plans for a holiday.' Lynn smiled as she nodded her agreement.

'Thank you. I told Assistant Matron that you wouldn't mind. You're always ready to step into the breach, aren't you? I don't know why you have accumulated a reputation, Nurse. I've never found you anything but willing and competent.'

'Thank you, Sister. Perhaps that's why you're always stuck with me,' retorted Lynn, and for a moment there was a trace of bitterness in her tone, for some of the Sisters had taken her reputation at its face value and treated her accordingly.

'That's not true, either. You're to take Nurse Atkinson's place in Children's. Go and report to Sister Wade, and give her my best wishes.'

'Yes, Sister.'

Lynn made her way through the hospital to the Children's Ward, which actually consisted of several wards. She liked Sister Wade, who was another sympathetic superior, and working with children had always appealed to Lynn, although she could never remain objective with younger patients and usually ended a tour of duty with a great deal of heartache.

'Ah, Nurse Avery!' commented Sister Wade, when Lynn reported. 'I heard you were coming. We have Nurses Tate and Barber on duty. Do you get along well with them?'

Lynn frowned at the question, but replied without hesitation.

'Yes, Sister, I get along with everyone.' She smiled inwardly at the thought, for none of the nurses liked Della Tate, whom they called the Porcelain Doll. Sophisticated and sleekly dark-haired, Nurse Tate was a menace to everyone who had hopes of attracting the male staff.

'Well, go and help Nurse Barber start the cleaning. The night staff have left the kitchen in a dreadful state.'

Lynn walked along the corridor and entered the kitchen, where Gwen Barber was already hard at work.

'Lynn!' exclaimed the girl, her pale eyes lighting up with pleasure. 'Are you here in Polly Atkinson's place?'

'That's right. Do you think you'll be able to cope with me around?'

'Come off it!' Gwen paused to subject Lynn to a closer scrutiny. 'They're not pinning something else on you, are they?'

'No. I was told when I came in that I'd have to postpone my holiday.'

'But you said you couldn't care less about holidays,' Gwen said. 'You're not still pining over your broken love affair, are you? That happened months ago.'

'It doesn't even enter my head now. I can see, with hindsight, that it would have been a disaster if it had gone as far as marriage. I was fortunate it broke up when it did.'

'But you haven't looked at a man since!'

'There's more to life than looking at men.'

'Perhaps, but there's nothing better!' Gwen smiled. 'I wish they'd look at me as much as they do at you.'

'Who?'

'The male staff! Don't try to kid me that you don't know Doctor Braddock is crazy about you.'

'He's asked me out enough times to make the point rather obvious, but Vince is not my idea of a nurse's dream come true.'

'It's all right for you. This is your home town. Your family lives here. But most of us are stuck in the Nurses' Home and we need a break after duty.'

Footsteps sounded in the corridor, and Gwen darted to the doorway and peered out, drawing back instantly and returning to Lynn's side. 'It's Doctor Morgan. There's a youngster on a trolley. Looks like a new admission.'

'Sister Wade will call for one of us if she needs us,' said Lynn, a frown upon her face as she saw the trolley pass the doorway, propelled by a porter. Doctor Morgan was walking beside the trolley, followed by a short, plump woman, who was clutching a boy's clothes in her arms. The small figure on the trolley was covered by a red blanket.

She turned back to her work, her expression suddenly taut, for seeing Paul Morgan had stirred an intangible emotion inside her. It was not the first time she had felt her pulses quicken at the sight of him.

She looked at her reflection in the stainless steel dish she was cleaning — blonde hair framing an attractive, heart-shaped face, but her blue eyes held a rather severe expression. Her crisp white cap was set firmly upon her curls and pinned there, and the starched uniform collar seemed to give her the appearance of a nun. Her lips twitched at the thought and she turned as Sister Wade peered in at the doorway.

'Nurse Barber, come with me!'

'How are you today?' demanded a cheery voice a few moments later, and she started slightly and glanced over a slender shoulder at the young man in a white coat whose fair, wavy hair looked the colour of straw. There was a smile on his fleshy face, and his blue eyes gleamed as he came into the big room.

'Hello, Vince,' responded Lynn, then shook her head. 'The answer is no before you ask.'

'I wish I knew what it was that Robert had. Outwardly, he didn't seem to be very much different to the rest of us, but he certainly hooked you, and dropped you heavily. But it's about time you got over that, Lynn.'

'You're not another one who thinks I'm suffering a broken heart, are you?'

'Aren't you?' he answered.

'Not at all! I've never felt happier! I'm certainly a lot wiser than I was a year ago, for instance.' A smile curved her lips but her eyes remained impassive, and Vince Braddock, looking into their cool depths, nodded slowly as he read the signs.

'All right, enough said. So you're off men for the time being. Well, I can wait. Just let me know when you're ready to pick up the pieces again.'

'I think you'll have a long wait,' she responded, returning to her work and ignoring him. The awkward ensuing pause was broken by a cool voice from the doorway.

'Hello, Vince! Not snooping around the female nursing staff again, are you? If Sister Wade catches you in here it won't be you who suffers but the nurse.'

Lynn turned her head and looked into the dark eyes of Della Tate, who lapsed quickly into silence at sight of her.

'Oh!' Della said softly. 'So we've been blighted, have we? I was hoping they'd send a nurse in place of Atkinson.'

'I'm as good a nurse as you, Della,'

responded Lynn in thin tones. 'In fact, I think I've proved that on more than one occasion.'

'Take it easy, girls,' implored Vince Braddock, moving quickly towards the door. 'Where's Doctor Morgan? I'm looking for him.'

'You'd hardly expect to find him in here, would you?' countered Della, looking pointedly at Lynn. 'Still, there's no accounting for taste, is there?'

Lynn smiled sweetly. 'You're just like a pill, Della,' she observed icily. 'You're coated with sugar, but very nasty inside. How did you get that way? Were you born like it or did you have to take lessons?'

Vince Braddock grinned nervously and departed. Della paused and surveyed Lynn, who returned the gaze with equal impassiveness before returning to her work. A few moments later, when Lynn glanced over her shoulder, she saw that Della had departed.

Gwen returned, and looked intently at Lynn.

'Did I see Della coming out of here?' she demanded, and frowned when Lynn nodded silently. 'What did she want? You two are like cat and dog.'

'Let's forget Della,' said Lynn. 'What about the new admission?'

'A boy aged four. Knocked over the saucepan his mother was using to boil eggs.'

Lynn clenched her teeth and shook her head slowly. 'Some mothers!' she commented. 'Is it bad?'

'Not as bad as they thought. He's lucky! Whopping blisters on him! They're putting him on a drip and one of the juniors is going to sit at his bedside. His mother is nearly frantic.'

Lynn dried her hands and began to put on her cuffs. 'I'd better report to Sister Wade. Is she in the ward?'

'She's talking to Doctor Morgan about the treatment for the new admission.' Gwen began to dry the dishes.

'I'll find her.' Lynn went into the corridor, and again felt that momentary fluttering of emotion in her breast and throat at sight of Paul Morgan standing talking with Sister Wade. She suppressed her feelings, telling herself sternly that he did not have the power to affect her. He was tall, dark and handsome, but that was all. His manner was rather stern, and he did not seem to flirt with the nurses like some of the other male staff. But it was rumoured that he had a fiancée in Wales, although he had been at the hospital three years now and did not seem to leave the town, even when he took his holidays.

'I've finished in the kitchen, Sister.'

'Sister, I think I would prefer a fully experienced nurse to sit with Jimmy Fielding,' cut in Doctor Morgan, his dark gaze holding Lynn's eyes. 'Nurse Avery is extremely competent, so I've heard.'

A ghost of a smile touched Sister Wade's lips, but she nodded without hesitation. 'Certainly, Doctor. I agree with you. Come along, Nurse. If you'll excuse me for a moment, Doctor.'

'I'll take her,' he said, and Sister Wade nodded her thanks and turned immediately to enter her office.

Lynn followed him into the ward, glancing around at the children in their beds. She had to harden her heart as she saw the small faces, some filled with wonder and some showing fear. She longed to comfort them all, to tell them that there was nothing to be afraid of and everything that was being done was for their good. Paul Morgan led her to the screened-off bed in a corner.

Taking over from the junior, she listened intently to the instructions, then settled herself down to watch the new admission. A glucose saline drip had been set up, the fluid entering his small body through a vein in his ankle. He was asleep now, out of his pain, under heavy sedation, and the slow drip continued monotonously. She made no sound, and with the screens drawn around the bed she felt isolated from the rest of the world.

Gwen relieved her an hour later, and

Lynn found Paul Morgan standing by the Sister's office as she approached. He eyed her as she paused and reported that there was no change in the patient's condition.

'Sister Wade has left the ward for a few minutes,' he said, as Lynn peered around his tall figure into the office. His voice held an impersonal tone, and Lynn glanced up into his face. He was always serious, as if he had a particular expression which he wore on duty.

'It's unusual to see you working in Children's, Doctor,' she commented, not wishing to stand silent beside him until Sister Wade returned. 'Aren't you always down in Casualty? I thought you specialised in accident cases.'

'They were busy down there when young Jimmy Fielding was brought in,' he commented. 'There was nothing I could do for him right then, except make him comfortable, so I brought him straight up. We'll see what condition he's in tomorrow.' He glanced along the corridor, then turned to her.

'Nurse, I've been looking for an opportunity to talk to you,' he said, in rather harsh tones, and smiled diffidently when he saw her quickly changing expression. 'You look as if you expect me to reprimand you,' he added. 'Do you have a guilty conscience?'

'No. it's just that I'm becoming accustomed to people blaming me for anything that goes wrong.'

'How did that start?'

'I don't know. But you know what they say about giving a dog a bad name.' Lynn paused, wanting to keep her distance and maintain the barriers she had set up in her mind. 'You wanted to speak to me?' she prompted.

'I've heard all the stories going the rounds about you, and I've noticed the way you look at times. I think you've got over the shock of losing Robert, but you're disillusioned, and if you don't make an effort to snap out of it, you could be burdened with a case of chronic depression, though I know it's none of my business.'

He paused again, frowning, and she spoke through clenched teeth: 'That's right, Doctor. It's nobody's business but my own.'

A shadow seemed to cross his face, and again he glanced around, but Lynn did not care if they were overheard.

'I didn't mean it to sound as if I were trying to interfere in your life,' he said quickly. 'As for it not being my business, perhaps it is as much mine as it is yours.'

She frowned as she looked into his eyes, again having to fight the pull of his magnetism. She shook her head. 'I don't understand,' she said.

'Nobody knows this, but Paula Wrenn and I had been seeing each other off duty, and it had begun to get serious. She went off with your ex-fiancé, so it does appear to put us in the same boat, you see. All I meant to do in bringing up the subject was to tell you that he wasn't worth ruining your personal life over. I recovered completely from Paula and I don't like to see you letting it get you down.'

'Oh!' Lynn was taken aback by his words, and he nodded slowly.

'I can understand why this has affected you worse than it did me,' he said. 'People talked about you because they knew everything. I was fortunate. They don't know about me.' He smiled thinly. 'They would have had a field day had they known. As it was, you took the full brunt of all the gossip. There's nothing they like better than a juicy scandal.'

'Well, I shan't breathe a word about you and Paula,' said Lynn seriously. 'And I can assure you, Doctor, that I'm not suffering from any complaint brought on by that scandal last year. In point of fact, I had begun to realise that Robert and I were not really suited, and now I view the whole matter with a great deal of relief.'

'But it has affected you, and I can clearly see it. Perhaps you don't realise it. That's why I spoke to you about it. Forgive me for broaching the subject, but you are still suffering from the business.'

'I'll take your word for it, if you insist. What do you suggest as a cure? Not another man!'

'Perhaps, perhaps not! I know Vince Braddock has been trying to entice you out.'

'He's fighting a losing battle. I like Vince, but I don't like his style.' Lynn saw Sister Wade coming along the corridor, carrying some X-ray plates, and she stiffened imperceptibly.

'Well, cheer up, at any rate,' he observed, also noticing the Sister. 'You're on holiday next week, aren't you?'

'No. It's been cancelled. One of the nurses is off with German measles, so I'm taking her place. But I wasn't looking forward to a holiday. I was supposed to be getting married.' Lynn shrugged. 'I'm glad its been cancelled. I'll wait until later in the year. We might have a good summer.'

Sister Wade arrived and spoke briskly.

'Nurse, you can take your break now. Fifteen minutes.'

'Yes, Sister.' Lynn glanced at Paul Morgan's face and a faint smile flitted across her lips. She went off along the corridor, and there was a strange sense of elation in her mind as she considered the short conversation she had had with the doctor. So he had been seeing Paula Wrenn! That was a juicy titbit the gossip-mongers would dearly love to secure, but they wouldn't get it from her. Lynn smiled cynically as she went down to the canteen. But the most enlightening thought in her mind was that Paul Morgan was human, after all. Behind that impassive exterior, there was a real man.

Returning to the ward after her break, she relieved Gwen at the bedside of Jimmy Fielding, and had the time and the opportunity to attempt self-analysis of the situation. She had to admit that she had become aware of Paul Morgan's existence, and that seemed to be the first step in a female's life to wanting to get to know a man better. But she wanted no entanglements, and discovered, upon trying to discard the train of thought, that it would not be discarded. Lynn felt disconcerted and indecisive, which was foreign to her nature.

She was glad when Gwen came to relieve her for lunch. But she didn't much feel like food, and went out to the car park to her small red car and drove homewards, mindful of the time, aware that the lunch-hour traffic would prevent her spending more than twenty minutes in the house.

She lived on the outskirts of town with her parents. Her father was a vet, and they lived in a very large house with twenty acres of land surrounding it, much of it grassland. Lynn had a horse, which she rode regularly, and also the pony her father had bought her when she was eight. Now twenty-four, she spent all her time divided between the hospital and her home, and most of her off-duty periods were spent on the land her father owned. She preferred the company of her horse and the solitude of the countryside.

When she reached home, it was almost time for her to start back, but she entered the large, grey-stone house and walked across the flagstoned hall to the big kitchen, where she surprised the housekeeper, Mrs. Moss, who started up from her lunch with an exclamation of horror.

'Lynn, you said you were not coming home to lunch!'

'Don't panic, Mrs. Moss,' declared Lynn with a smile. 'You'll give yourself indigestion. I haven't come home to lunch. I just wanted to get away from the hospital, that's all.'

'Have they been getting at you again?' Mrs. Moss was tall and thin, a faithful woman who had been housekeeper at Fairfields since before Lynn was born.

'No. It has been a pleasant morning, actually.' Lynn smiled at some of her recollections. 'But my holiday has been postponed. One of the married nurses has a young daughter who's just come down with German measles. We're so short-staffed that I've got to take her place in the Children's Ward.'

'I think you need a change!' Mrs. Moss said. 'It would do you good to work away from home for a spell. But let me get you something to eat. You can't go all day with nothing.'

'I'll get myself a sandwich. You finish your meal.' Lynn went to the larder, and chatted as she prepared herself a snack. 'Has Father been home to lunch? This is his day for the country round, and it is Friday today, isn't it?'

'That's right. Don't tell me you've even forgotten what day it is.' Mrs. Moss looked perturbed as she continued her interrupted meal. 'You really needed that holiday, Lynn.'

'I'll have it when the weather is more settled.' Lynn ate her skimpy meal and then departed to return to the hospital.

When she walked into the ward, she discovered Doctor Morgan at the far end. He was talking to Gwen Barber, but left her immediately he saw Lynn and came towards her. She studied his handsome face as he approached, and thought he seemed rather angry.

'Would you mind stepping out into the corridor for a moment, Nurse?' he requested.

Lynn frowned and followed him. She glanced at the window of the Sister's office which looked into the ward, and was thankful that Sister Wade was not there. When they paused in the corridor, she looked inquiringly into his face.

'Nurse, when I spoke to you this morning it was in the strictest confidence,' he said heavily.

'Naturally,' she agreed. 'They would have a field day if they managed to get hold of information like that.'

'They have got hold of it! When I went to lunch, it was flung in my face.' His eyes were glittering with anger, and Lynn caught her breath as the import of his words sunk into her mind.

'But you don't think I said anything to anyone, do you?' she faltered.

'I've never told another living soul about it,' he retorted. 'If you didn't mention the fact, then how do you account for such a coincidence? I told you about it this morning and word of it gets out the same day.' His tone was low-pitched, but there was contempt in his voice which cut Lynn to the quick.

'But I haven't seen anyone to talk to,' she answered, shaking her head. 'I went home for lunch. I've only just come back. Apart from that, I'm not in the habit of gossiping, Doctor!'

'If you didn't spread it, then who did?' he asked.

'How do I know? Perhaps we were overheard this morning. In this hospital, even the walls have ears!' Lynn stalked around him and went to the kitchen, peering inside, and saw Della there, a smug grin on her attractive face. Della pulled a face at her, and Lynn returned to where Morgan was standing. 'I think your answer is standing in the kitchen now,' she said sharply. 'Nurse Tate! She was probably in the kitchen this morning, and she would do anything to get me into trouble.'

He sighed heavily, shaking his head as he regarded her. For a moment longer, he was stiff with anger. Then he made a visible effort to relax, and forced a grin.

'Oh, what the devil!' he said. 'It doesn't matter, anyway. It's all so much water under the bridge, isn't it?'

'The affair might be, but accusing me of a breach of confidence is another matter,' snapped Lynn angrily.

'I apologise!' He shrugged his wide shoulders. 'What was I to think?'

'You think along the same wavelength as everyone else at the hospital,' she retorted. 'I'm getting tired of being blamed for everything that goes wrong around here.'

'I can't say any more than I'm sorry,' he told her flatly. 'Forget it, it doesn't matter.'

'It matters enough for you to accuse me as soon as I show my face on the ward!'

'It wasn't that so much, not what was said. But the thought that you had betrayed my confidence hurt me. I was under the impression that you're a great deal different to most of the nurses here. You're not like the rest. At least, that's how you seemed to me.'

'I'm certainly not like the rest of them. You have only to talk to any of the Ward Sisters and they'll tell you that. I'm the one who plays all the tricks on the staff.' Lynn fought against her anger, but it bubbled up powerfully.

'Good grief!' he said in low tones. 'You're like a volcano that's erupted. Do you want me to go down on my knees and apologise?'

Lynn swallowed and gritted her teeth. 'For two pins, I'd quit nursing,' she said sharply.

'Is it as bad as that?' He looked concerned now. 'It isn't just our little misunderstanding is it? You're really at the end of your patience.'

'It will pass. I'll get over it. I'm sorry, Doctor!' She felt her anger subsiding, and suddenly realised how ridiculous she must look. If Sister Wade returned and overheard her having an altercation with a doctor she would be on the carpet in no uncertain manner.

'No, I said I'm sorry, and I'm to blame. I ought to have kept my mouth shut this morning, and I don't believe that you said anything about that business.'

'Thank you for that much,' she said huffily, and suddenly he was grinning.

'You're a very beautiful girl when you're angry,' he commented. 'It's the first time I've seen you acting almost human in months. Perhaps there's hope for you, after all!'

'I don't understand, Doctor — ' Lynn heard footsteps along the corridor and glanced around to see Sister Wade approaching — 'I must get into the ward and do something.'

'Take over at Jimmy Fielding's

bedside,' he said, 'although he won't need watching much longer. He's settling down and the shock is receding. Let's go and look at him, shall we?'

Lynn drew a long, ragged breath as she followed him into the ward, and a sense of unreality seemed to grip her. She had been almost shouting at him. Whatever must he think?

Gwen stood up as they entered the bed area, and the remnants of Lynn's anger fled as she looked down on the blistered body of Jimmy Fielding. She watched Morgan's long, gentle fingers as he felt for the boy's pulse, and he smiled at her as he met her gaze.

Sister Wade appeared, catching Morgan's eye, and he nodded slowly. They moved away from the bed and Lynn heard Morgan say that the boy could be left but checked every fifteen minutes.

'Come along then,' said Sister Wade, glancing at Lynn and Gwen. 'Let's get some work done, shall we?'

Lynn saw a faint smile on Morgan's face as she departed, and she felt confused. As she and Gwen left the ward, her colleague glanced at her.

'I heard your voice right in the ward,' she accused. 'You weren't shouting at Doctor Morgan, surely?'

'We had a slight difference of opinion.' There was a gleam in Lynn's eyes. 'But I'm going to watch our for Della in future. If she so much as looks like trying to get me into trouble I'll take her to task.'

'What happened?' demanded Gwen.

'Why do you want to know?' Lynn asked sharply. 'Do you want to spread it around?' She saw the protest in the girl's expression and smiled apologetically. 'Sorry, Gwen, but that's how I'm feeling right now. Nothing seems to be going right.'

'Does it ever for you?'

'That's a good question. I think I've been a fool over the past months and, because of it, everyone has been taking me for granted. I think I'll make an effort to change my image.'

'What are you going to do? Don't get

into trouble, Lynn, it isn't worth it.'

'Trouble? I never get into trouble.' Lynn went into the kitchen, where Della was about to depart. 'Not unless someone pushes me into it, eh, Della?'

'Are you accusing me?' demanded Della, as she shouldered past.

'The guilty never need accusing,' snapped Lynn. She smiled at the worried expression on Gwen's face. Della left, and as the girl's footsteps receded, Lynn unclenched her hands, filled with intangible emotions that threatened to overwhelm her. 'Do you know something?' she demanded of the startled Gwen. 'I feel like breaking away from the old routine. If Vince Braddock came in here now and asked me to go out with him I might even say yes.'

'Would you say 'yes' to me, if I asked you?' demanded Paul Morgan, and Lynn spun around to see him standing in the doorway, a quizzical expression in his dark eyes.

Gwen's mouth gaped, and her eyes

widened. Lynn glanced at her colleague, aware that this very conversation would be repeated all over the hospital.

'Why, Doctor, if you asked me I'd certainly say 'yes'.' Lynn smiled wickedly, her eyes gleaming. 'Don't you know that most of the eligible nurses in the hospital are just waiting for you to snap your fingers? But what about Nurse Tate? Della has laid odds that if anyone can date you, she can.'

'So I've heard,' he retorted softly. 'That's why I'm asking you. Would you care to go out with me this evening, Nurse Avery?'

'Thank you for asking. Yes, I would like to, very much.' Lynn smiled as she spoke, and although there was a flippant tone in her voice, her eyes were most serious. She gravely held his gaze, saw him nod slowly, and heard Sister Wade's heavy footsteps in the background along the corridor.

'Sister's coming,' cut in Gwen anxiously.

'I'll be waiting by my car when you

get off duty,' said Paul Morgan quickly. 'We can make arrangements then. Thank you, Nurse. You've just made my day. Vince Braddock has been bragging about how he would be the first man to take you out, and it seems that I've beaten him to the punch.'

'I feel just as happy, putting a spoke in Della's wheel,' retorted Lynn, and he smiled and departed unhurriedly.

'Good heavens!' said Gwen, moving instinctively to appear busy when Sister Wade looked into the room. 'The way you talked to him! Lynn, you're the giddy limit! But wait until I put this around! You'll hear Della screaming in mortification all over the hospital!'

'That's the only reason I'm going out with him, Gwen,' retorted Lynn. 'I want to spite Della.'

'What a date it will be,' commented Gwen, shaking her head. 'Neither of you is keen to go out. You're just getting together to spite other people! I've never heard anything like it.'

2

When she went off duty, Lynn found Paul Morgan standing beside her car, and some of the nurses going off her shift were loitering in the background, watching. She saw Gwen Barber and her friend, Chrissie, and moving across the yard towards the gate that led to the adjacent Nurses' Home was Della Tate. Seeing Della killed the apprehension in Lynn's mind, and she smiled cheerfully when she confronted Paul.

'Doctor,' she said lightly, 'you shouldn't be here waiting for me. You're making it appear that you're anxious to see me, and half my colleagues are watching us right now.'

'That's right.' He nodded, catching her mood and smiling. 'That's why I'm out here and acting like an expectant father waiting outside a labour ward. If they want something to talk about then

'I'll give it to them. Do you know that Vince Braddock button-holed me a few minutes ago and demanded to know if there was some truth in the rumour that I have a date with you?'

'So soon?' She chuckled merrily, her blue eyes gleaming. 'That will be Gwen's work. Della is a nasty type and all the nurses would love to see Della taken down a peg or two. Ah, she's just spotted us together!'

'So I see, but it doesn't really matter what others think. I've asked you out because I would like to have your company. I don't want you to agree to go out with me merely to spite your colleagues. At least have an ounce of desire for my company.'

'But I do have, Doctor!' Lynn laughed. 'The dishy Doctor Morgan figures in every good nurse's dreams. I'm quite looking forward to spending an evening in your company. Where are you going to take me?'

'Where would you like to go?' he countered.

'I don't know. I've got out of the habit of going out for the evening. I have come to prefer solitude. But anything you care to suggest will suit me.'

'What do you usually do in the evenings?' he asked.

'Ride my horse, or go with my father on his call-outs.' She paused. 'My father is a vet.'

'I know. I took the trouble to find out all about you a long time ago.' A smile touched his lips when he saw the surprise that flickered across her face. 'I even took the trouble to locate your home, and the other evening I saw you out riding. I used to ride, but that was a long time ago. There isn't a riding stable conveniently placed to this town or I would have kept it up.'

'Would you care to come to my home this evening then? I think you'd be a bit heavy for my horse, but Father has several horses and I'm sure he wouldn't mind you riding one of them. In fact, he might appreciate that. It would save him time in exercising some of them.'

'That sounds like a very good idea. You've got quite a large place on the outskirts of town, haven't you?'

'Twenty acres.'

'About the size of the place my father owned in Wales,' he remarked. 'It's strange, but I lived under similar conditions to you. I miss all that.'

'Then why are you working in England?' she asked curiously. 'They have hospitals in Wales, don't they?'

'My father was killed in a road accident four years ago, and my mother died of a broken heart within the year. I moved out to forget, and I haven't been back. My brother lives on the family estate. He has become insistent over the past year about my return, but I don't think I can face it.'

'I'm sorry,' she said softly. 'So that's why you've seemed sad sometimes. A lot of girls thought you had experienced a broken romance.'

'That's the obvious line of speculation.' He nodded and glanced around.

'Now what about this evening? We're making quite a spectacle of ourselves, standing here.'

'Who cares?' she retorted. 'We're off duty.' A glance in the direction where the nurses had been standing showed her that Chrissie and Gwen were leading the others towards the Nurses' Home, and she could imagine the thread of their conversation.

'Our audience is departing,' he remarked good-naturedly. 'Shall I drive out to your home this evening?'

'Please do,' Lynn agreed. 'I think you'd like to meet my parents. My father would be interested in you. Then I'll show you around the place, and you can see my horse and pony.'

'Sounds like a nice way to spend an evening. What time shall I appear?'

'Any time you like after seven.' There was a lightness in Lynn's tone which belied the tension in her mind.

She drove home steadily, following the stream of rush-hour traffic, and her thoughts were upon Paul Morgan. It was strange how the events of the day had developed, but she sensed that the hand of Fate was at work, and resigned herself to the fact as she drove up to the house and parked behind her father's old estate car, which he used for his business.

Entering the house, she peeped into the lounge to find her mother watching the news on TV. Mrs. Avery was tall and slim, a vivacious woman in her early fifties who had worked in her husband's business for thirty years. She handled the animal clinic in the town and took care of the administration. She had been a nurse at the Stokeford General before marrying, and left to work with sick animals instead of people.

'Hello, Lynn,' she greeted, her grey eyes lighting up as she surveyed her only daughter. 'You're looking rather pleased with yourself. What have you been up to today?'

'Mother, you sound just like the Sisters at the hospital,' protested Lynn, smiling good-naturedly. 'Every time I look happy, they want to know what I've been up to. Well, I haven't put a foot wrong today, which must seem like a record to you. Are you going out this evening?'

'No, dear. Father wants to go riding. He never gets enough time to exercise the horses, and I'm going out for some fresh air, but we'll be around. Why?'

Lynn explained about Paul Morgan, and Mrs. Avery's eyes took on an even brighter expression.

'Now don't jump to conclusions,' said Lynn firmly. 'I only agreed to see him because I knew it would spite Della Tate. She's been boasting about how she'll be the first nurse to attract our Doctor Morgan, and I've beaten her to it. She'll never live it down, and it's about time something was done about her. I feel sure she's to blame for all the trouble they've held me responsible for.'

'But that isn't the best reason for seeing a young man,' protested Mrs. Avery. 'I don't know what your generation is coming to, Lynn. You wouldn't lead him up the garden path, would you?'

'Don't be old-fashioned, Mother.' Lynn chuckled lightly. 'I learned today that Paul Morgan was seeing Nurse Wrenn before she took Robert away from me. That's the only thing Paul and I have in common, and when he asked me to see him I thought it would make a pleasant change. He comes from Wales originally, and lived on a place like this. It might cheer him up if Father would let him ride one of the horses. He misses that sort of thing.'

'I'm sure Father would be delighted to have his help. There seems to be less and less time available to us as the days pass.'

'I know what you mean. Where is Father? I'd better have a word with him, then change. Paul will be here just after seven.'

'Does he know where to come?'

'Yes.' Lynn paused on her way to the door. 'It seems that he has taken the trouble to find out. He's a most surprising man.'

She thought about him as she went up to her room and stripped off her uniform. Pulling on a dressing-gown, she went into the bathroom and took a shower, then dressed in jeans and a sweater. When she went down to the kitchen, she found her father seated at the big table, eating abstractedly while reading the newspaper. He looked up quickly when she paused and kissed his forehead, and a smile broke out on his rugged, weatherbeaten face.

'Hello, Lynn,' he greeted. 'What kind of a day have you had?' He was tall and well fleshed, with sandy-coloured hair and blue eyes.

'Can't grumble,' she replied, slipping into a seat next to him and smiling as Mrs. Moss placed a salad before her. 'You're going riding this evening, so Mother said.'

'Must take the time to give the horses some exercise,' he retorted, folding the paper and giving her his whole attention. 'What about you? Will you ride one of my animals for a change?'

'I'll ride Goldy,' she said, 'but I have a friend coming over after tea who'll help you out. He's a doctor.' She began to explain about Paul, and saw her father's appreciative nod.

'Fine. We'll see what kind of a rider he is first, of course, but if you have anyone else at the hospital who can ride and fancies that kind of relaxation off duty then bring them home. I haven't the time these days to ride as much as I'd like, and I don't want to have to get rid of any of the horses.'

'Oh, no!' agreed Lynn, frowning. She began to eat, and was thoughtful for a moment.

'Are you interested in this chap?' asked her father, stirring his tea.

'No.' Lynn smiled as she recounted the events of her day, and her father's face was set in serious lines as he regarded her.

'I don't know who you take after,' he said when she lapsed into silence.

'You're not irresponsible, but there's some strange quirk in your nature which makes you appear impetuous. It must weigh against you at the hospital. Why don't you consider giving up nursing and come to work with me? I could do with your help.'

'No, thanks.' Lynn shook her head and, for a moment, her blue eyes were extremely serious. 'As much as I like animals, I think that people should have the benefit of my training. I am a good nurse, despite what some people at the hospital think. I'll stay where I am, thank you. But I'll help you out on my day off, if you like.'

'No. You need your free time. I know just how demanding your job is. But next week you could help on the odd day. You won't know what to do with your time after a few days.'

'Sorry, Dad, but my holiday has been postponed!' She smiled. 'I'm relieved, in a way.'

Mrs. Avery entered the kitchen as she spoke, and paused in the doorway. 'You didn't cancel it yourself, did you?' she demanded.

'No.' Lynn explained the reasons, and her mother nodded.

'You've forgotten all about Robert now, haven't you?' she asked gently.

'I don't suppose I shall ever forget him,' replied Lynn seriously. 'But he doesn't hurt me any more. I can think of him and not feel anything at all.'

'Time is a great healer,' remarked her father, setting down his cup and rising from the table. 'What time is your friend arriving? I'll be in the stables.'

'I'll bring him around when he shows up. I told him not before seven, knowing that you sometimes get in late.'

'And I may be called out,' came the immediate reply. 'There's a cow due to calve at Richmond's farm, and I didn't like her condition when I saw her. They'll call if there are complications. You'll find me close to the house if there are any telephone messages, Mrs. Moss.'

'It would make a change if you weren't called out,' said Mrs. Avery. 'I'll go and change into my riding gear and join you.'

'I'll wait for Paul,' said Lynn, glancing at the clock. 'He should be arriving in fifteen minutes. If I know anything about him he'll be punctual.'

'Has he been at the hospital long?' asked Mrs. Avery, as her husband departed by way of the kitchen door.

'Several years. He's always remained aloof, and gave the impression of being the type who likes solitude. But he told me a thing or two about himself this afternoon and I can understand how he feels. It will do him good to come here now and again.'

'So you are concerned about him,' suggested Mrs. Avery.

'Not in the least. But he'll be able to help Father exercise the horses, and it'll take him out of himself. He seems to need that.'

'Well, I can't wait to meet him,' responded her mother, smiling. 'Any man who can make you think twice is worth meeting.'

Lynn smiled, but she sat as if on thorns while the minute hand of the clock moved on towards the hour, and when the front doorbell rang, she sprang up as Mrs. Moss went forward to answer.

'I'll get it, Mrs. Moss,' she said, and the housekeeper merely smiled and went on with her work.

Lynn took a deep breath as she prepared to open the front door. She could see the dark shape of a tall figure standing outside and knew that it was Paul Morgan.

'Good evening, Doctor,' she greeted him.

'Well!' he declared, gazing at her with undisguised surprise. 'I wouldn't have believed it possible. They say that clothes maketh man, but Nurse Avery out of uniform is a sight to behold.'

Lynn glanced down at herself, taking in the crumpled jeans and the sweater, then she looked at him, casually dressed in dark-brown trousers and an open-necked check shirt.

'You look more like a Canadian lumberjack than a hospital doctor,' she stated. 'But it's a change for the better in your case, I'd say. You look more human, especially without the white coat.'

'Thank you. I'm sure you're being complimentary, but how is it you always manage to make it sound as if I'm being insulted?'

'Do I?' She smiled disarmingly. 'Come in and meet Mrs. Moss, our housekeeper. Mother and Father are out at the stables, but Mrs. Moss is the most important person in the household.'

They went through to the kitchen, and Mrs. Moss subjected him to a close scrutiny when Lynn introduced him. The old housekeeper nodded approvingly behind Paul's back as Lynn continued to the back door, and Lynn set her teeth firmly, for she had no intention of giving anyone the impression that she was getting interested in this handsome doctor.

Her parents were saddling up when they reached the stables, and Lynn watched Paul's reactions as she introduced him. He shook hands with Mrs. Avery, glancing at Lynn as he did so, and spoke gently.

'It's easy to see where Lynn gets her good looks from, Mrs. Avery,' he said.

'It's nice to meet a pleasant flatterer,' replied Lynn's mother.

'I'm very interested in your work,' Paul told Lynn's father, and went on to explain that he had almost decided to become a vet when he first planned his career.

'Father has asked me to consider giving up nursing and help him in his business,' interposed Lynn, and saw Paul glance quickly at her.

'Good nurses are hard to find,' he responded. 'But don't let that influence you. Do whatever will make you happiest.'

'That's good advice,' said Lynn's

father. 'Come and take a look at my horses. Lynn tells me you can ride. You'll be welcome to come here at any time and take out any of our animals. They can do with all the exercise they can get.'

'Thank you,' Paul accepted eagerly. 'I've ransacked my wardrobe to find the most suitable clothes.'

'You could get yourself a pair of jeans to go with that shirt,' observed Lynn with a smile, and was rewarded with a grin. 'The nurses should see you now,' she added.

Mrs. Avery glanced disapprovingly at Lynn, who followed her father and Paul into the stable. She went to the stall where her pony, Samson was waiting, and patted him before going on to Goldy, her chestnut mare. By the time she had saddled and bridled Goldy, Paul was leading her father's grey gelding out into the evening sunlight, and he was patting the animal, making friends with it. She watched with interest as he mounted, and she quickly saw that Paul was an accomplished rider. He went off at a canter, and Lynn hurriedly mounted and took off in pursuit, catching up with him some fifty yards from the stable. They followed a path that led right across the grassland.

The sunlight was warm, although the ground was heavy, for the recent rain had caused the grass to grow luxuriously. Spring was finally in the air, decided Lynn, as she gazed around, breathing deeply of the clean air. The familiar scenery seemed sharper, as if her mind has suddenly slipped into focus after a period of confusion. When she glanced sideways at Paul, she guessed that getting to know him was the real reason for her sudden change. She smiled as he looked at her, his teeth flashing in a grin.

'This is more like it,' he remarked. 'You don't know how lucky you are, having a home like this. I only wish I'd plucked up courage before this to ask you out.'

'You needed courage to ask me out?'

she queried, filled with surprise.

'Why used that tone? Don't you think I am human?'

'I think you're are going to surprise a lot of the nurses,' she retorted. 'None of them thinks you're a lesser mortal.'

'I'm not concerned by what they think. But you're a very surprising girl, Lynn.'

'Oh?' She noted his use of her first name, and it seemed to come easily from his tongue. 'What's surprising about me?'

'Seeing you out of uniform makes you look less clinical.' He grinned as she started. 'Now don't start lashing me with that tongue of yours,' he protested. 'You're an outspoken creature and it is a quality I like in a woman. But you can overdo it sometimes. It can be overdone, you know.'

She stifled the retort which rose to her lips, shaking her head instead, and they rode on steadily across the series of meadows. There was a stream cutting across the land at an angle, and when

Paul reined in, Lynn halted and dismounted. He looked down at her.

'There's only one thing missing to make this the perfect setting,' he commented.

'What's that?'

'Mountains.' He dismounted and held the reins of the grey, coming to her side. 'Now if there was a mountain over there instead of the town this would be my idea of heaven.'

'You're a strange man,' she said, and he glanced at her. 'You're not at all the type I imagined.'

'Don't tell me you're guilty of judging people an appearances!' he mocked with a smile, and she nodded slowly.

'I always thought you were moody, but you've explained the reason for that. But there was more to it. I had the impression, too, that you didn't want to mix with anyone at the hospital. There again, I was wrong because you were seeing — ' She broke off as his face hardened in its expression.

'Perhaps we'd better forget that business of the past,' he said. 'It won't help to bring it up.'

'You're right, of course, but being out here with you now has jogged my memory. The last time I was out in a man's company it was with Robert.'

'Did he come riding with you?'

'Robert?' She chuckled as she shook her head. 'He wasn't the type. He would rather have sat watching TV! I knew before the break came that he wasn't the man for me. It showed in lots of ways. I was relieved, I think, although the way the break occurred shocked me. But, generally, it was only my pride that was hurt. Nobody at the hospital appreciates that fact. They still think I'm moping around.'

'Let them think what they like. I felt the same way from my side, but, as I told you, I recovered quite quickly. Now it is all over, and I think we'd better accept it.'

'I accepted it a long time ago.'

'Then don't talk about it again.'

There was a rebuke in his tone, and Lynn sighed heavily as she regarded him. But he turned to look at the stream, and the silence that pressed in about them was perfect except for the noise of the running water. 'Are there fish in the stream?' he asked.

'Yes. Father loves fishing, but he doesn't find the time for it these days. What about you?'

'I used to fish in the old days, before I left home.' There was a trace of sadness in his tone and he did not look at her. 'I don't think I'd care to start it again.' He turned slowly to take in the scenery. 'Were you born here?' he demanded.

'Yes.' She was surprised by his question.

'Then you're an extremely fortunate girl, Lynn.'

'I know that!' He had moved closer to her, and for a moment their arms touched. Lynn felt an electric pulse cut through her. She moved away from him, suddenly disconcerted, and felt confused, for her heart seemed to be trying to thud its way through her rib cage. Compressing her lips, she swung back into the saddle, then gazed down at him as he studied her. 'We're supposed to be exercising these horses,' she said firmly. 'Come on, I'll race you back to the stable.'

Before he could remount, she had urged Goldy away, and the mare galloped along the path. Exhilaration filled Lynn as the wind tugged at her curls, and she felt herself come alive for the first time in many months. It was as if the winter had finally been chased out of her heart.

By the time darkness came, Lynn was tired, but strangely elated. Her parents had already gone into the house, and she lingered after she and Paul had completed putting away the tack. When they went out into the open, the sun was slipping away behind the horizon, leaving a crimson sky and limning the small, fleecy clouds with golden fire. Shadows were creeping in from the fields, and a faint mist seemed to rise up from the sodden ground. It gave the atmosphere a ghostly unreal appearance, and she stifled a sigh as she looked around.

'It's been a long time since I saw a real sunset in a rural setting,' he exclaimed, and she glanced up at his shadowed face to see a sombre expression on his features.

'Are you basically a sad man?' she asked quietly. 'What is it about you, Paul? Are you looking back into the past instead of living in the present?'

'You seem to know all about that sort of thing,' he countered without hesitation. 'Is that what you do?'

'No. I passed through that phase some time ago, and it's behind me now. I think it's more difficult for a man, if he is forced into it, to escape from it. Perhaps that's what I sense about you.'

'You should have studied psychiatry!' His tone was brusque, but his teeth glinted as he smiled.

'There's a little bit of the psychiatrist

in all of us,' she replied, 'and some of us need the help of fully-trained psychiatrists, judging by the antics of certain of my colleagues.'

'What about you? This reputation you've gained. I can't believe that it is deserved because you're such an efficient nurse. Why do you accept what they say without objection?'

'It doesn't matter to me what anyone thinks. I suspect Della of being the cause of my reputation. She hates me intensely for some reason, and I believe she was responsible for those japes that were attributed to me. But, at the time, I was prepared to accept the blame because it kept everyone talking about those escapades instead of about Robert.'

'I see. But now you're got over the Robert affair, you're still stuck with this unfortunate reputation, and that won't do your career any good.'

'Do you think I worry about that?' Lynn chuckled. 'I'm quite content to remain as I am. Who wants to rise to the dizzy heights of Sister? Nursing is in my blood and nursing is what I'm doing. That's what really counts with me.'

'So you're a regular Florence Nightingale! One wouldn't think that, listening to the tales about you.'

'You must have been listening quite closely,' she retorted. 'You even found out where I live. What's the interest?'

'You're blunt, Lynn, and it's disconcerting at times.' He considered his answer before replying. 'Supposing I told you I'd heard about this place your father owned out here, and as I liked the outdoors life and there were horses to ride here, I decided to cultivate your friendship in order to angle an invitation to visit. Would you be offended or would you prefer that explanation to something more personal?'

'I don't quite know how to take that.' She smiled slowly, shaking her head. 'But come into the house and have a drink. No doubt you'll be able to get around my father as easily as you conned me, and he'll let you come over when you wish. Actually, I am glad there's nothing personal in your interest in me. I don't want you to get any ideas about me, and I have no wish to go through all that again.'

'My sentiments entirely.' He turned away, and Lynn accompanied him to the house.

When they entered, Mrs. Avery called from the lounge, and Paul followed Lynn into the long room.

'Come in and sit down, Paul,' invited Mrs. Avery.

'Where's Father?' asked Lynn, as she and Paul went to sit down.

'Called out, I'm afraid. It's the same old story.'

'One has to be dedicated to this type of work,' agreed Paul. 'It happens all the time at the hospital. But you were a nurse, Mrs. Avery, so you know what it's like.'

'Only too well. And from what Lynn has said about you, I suspect that you don't get enough relaxation. My husband has told me to invite you whenever you like. I don't expect he'll be back before you go, so please do take advantage of the invitation.'

'He will,' said Lynn with conviction, but there was a smile upon her lips to take the sting out of her words, although Mrs. Avery looked a bit surprised. But Paul laughed and nodded.

'Thank you,' he replied. 'If I don't grate upon Lynn's nerves too much, I'd like nothing better than to come now and again.' He launched into an account of his early life in Wales, of the countryside in which he had lived and his love for it. 'This is the nearest I've been to home since I left,' he ended. 'The only thing lacking here are mountains, as I told Lynn.'

'I'll see what I can do about that before your next visit,' cut in Lynn, chuckling, and he grinned.

He stayed until ten-thirty, and Lynn saw him to the door when he intimated that he ought to depart. He looked at her with a gleam in his dark eyes and a smile on his face.

'Thank you for an entertaining evening,' he said. 'It was like taking a trip back home, as it used to be.'

'Well, you have an open invitation, so you can make that trip any time you feel like it, even when I'm not here. Father really would appreciate it if you came and rode some of the horses, but don't ever climb on the back of my Goldy, will you?'

'I wouldn't dream of touching anything that belonged to you,' he replied with mock gravity. 'I'm sure that if I did, you'd bite off my head. I feel fortunate that I've escaped in one piece this evening, so I'll bid you good night. I'll probably see you at the hospital tomorrow.'

'There will be a lot of talk about us tomorrow,' she prophesied.

'You're the original 'I-don't-care-girl', aren't you?'

'That's right. It doesn't matter what

they say. But I'll be eager to see Della's face in the morning, and I won't be able to resist rubbing it in when I get the chance.'

'Don't pile it on too thick,' he protested. 'I have to work there, remember, and if you start spreading tall stories about our torrid evening together, I'll be gaining an unsavoury reputation. They seem quick to hand them out, don't they?'

He shook his head and turned away, and Lynn watched him depart. When he had gone, she felt a trace of loneliness filtering through her mind, and sighed heavily as she closed the door and went back into the lounge.

'Well, it's been hectic, listening to you cutting Paul to pieces, and he trying to defend himself,' remarked Mrs. Avery. 'He must be one of the best-natured men living, the way he suffers your attacks. What's come over you, Lynn? You never used to be like that. Is it because of Robert?'

'Never! I don't miss Robert. I'm

relieved it turned out the way it did.'

'Then it must be a subconscious thing. I think you're afraid to be your normal gentle self for fear you should fall in love again. You're instinctively making yourself nasty to Paul to scare him off.'

'He'll take some scaring off.' Lynn smiled thinly. 'He doesn't care about me and made it clear today before asking me out. He just wanted to come here. He's lonely, and homesick, I believe. He heard about this place and figures he could be happy here with the horses.'

'Well, that could be the answer. He wouldn't come if he felt anything for you. Your manner would kill an elephant at twenty yards. I'd tone it down a little if I were you, dear. He's such a nice person, and all he wants is to be friendly.'

'I don't feel the need for a male friend,' Lynn retorted. 'I'm going to bed now. I have to be up early in the morning. Good night, Mother.'

In the sanctuary of her room, Lynn sat at her dressing-table and regarded herself in the big, circular mirror, trying to sort out her mixed feelings. She had looked forward to Paul's company, despite her sharp attitude towards him, and although she had pretended to like his attitude towards her — impersonal and just friendly — she inwardly protested against it.

3

She went to bed with a smile on her lips, and the sound of Paul's voice seemed to haunt her dreams. Next morning, she rose early, and found herself humming lightly as she prepared for duty. When she drove into the hospital, Paul's car was already there, and she saw the day-staff nurses hurrying into the building.

Reality faced her as she entered the main doors and went along to Children's. Her footsteps sounded determined in the corridor, but inside she was suddenly feeling apprehensive. She had put on a brazen attitude the evening before, and now she might have to pay for that.

Chrissie was just ahead of her, obviously waiting for her before going on to Women's Medical, and the girl's dark eyes were bright with curiosity as she studied Lynn's impassive expression.

'Well, how did it go?' she asked eagerly, as Lynn paused before her. 'For once, you're the heroine of the hospital, Lynn. Poor Della was ragged unmercifully in the Home. She won't live that down in a hurry. But what about you and Paul Morgan?'

'What about us?' replied Lynn, poker-faced. 'We went out for the evening. There's nothing in that, surely?'

'You know what I mean! Don't play the innocent. Paul Morgan hasn't glanced twice at a nurse since he's been here, and you haven't looked at another man since Robert. Then suddenly, out of the blue, the two of you are going out together.'

'One swallow doesn't make a summer,' quoted Lynn. 'I must go, Chrissie, or I'll be late.'

'Well, look out for Della after this. She was so certain that Paul Morgan was interested in her! She's a spiteful female, and she might try to get back at you.'

'Now you're really worrying me.' Lynn grinned. 'See you later.'

'Lynn!' At Gwen Barber's call, Lynn turned and waited for her colleague to catch up with her. There was a smile on the girl's face, and she took hold of Lynn's arm as they continued.

'You look as if you expect to be given a whole list of lurid details,' commented Lynn.

'Well, what happened?' demanded Gwen. 'You're the very limit, Lynn, you know that. First of all, you were shouting at Doctor Morgan, then he's asking you to go out with him.'

'It just proves that you have to stand up to these people, doesn't it?' Lynn smiled.

'Watch out for Della this morning. If she can make trouble for you she'll do it. She was furious last night, and the girls made it far worse by ragging her about it. She was so certain that she was going to be the first to have the pleasure of Doctor Morgan's company.'

'It's about time she was put in her place.' Lynn began to clear her mind of personal thoughts as they approached the Sister's office, and Sister Wade was standing in the entrance to the main ward, already at work checking her charges. She glanced around at the sound of their footsteps, and a smile appeared briefly upon her face.

'Hello, girls,' she greeted. 'Nurse Barber, would you show Nurse Jameson around? Nurse Avery, I want you to start cleaning the kitchen. The night staff haven't done a thing.'

Lynn nodded and turned aside immediately, entering the kitchen where breakfast dishes were piled high, and she paused, a sparkle coming to her eyes when she saw Della already at work at the sink, her cuffs off and steam rising up around her. Lynn wondered if Sister Wade had deliberately put them together, but knew her superior well enough to know that the only thought in Sister Wade's mind was the efficient running of the department.

'Hello, Della,' she greeted as she prepared to start drying, and her smile widened as Della glanced at her. 'It's a lovely morning, isn't it?'

'You may think so,' came the ominous retort, and Della plunged into her work with unaccustomed energy.

'I don't often listen to the rumours that go the rounds of the hospital, or the gossip,' continued Lynn, 'but I couldn't help hearing something of what's happening at the moment. Is it true that you were wagering you'd be the first to go out with Paul Morgan?'

'Just talk! I'm not interested in Paul Morgan or any other doctor in the hospital. I've got my sights set rather higher than their level.'

'Bully for you!' Lynn smiled as she began to dry the dishes. 'But I'll set your mind at rest, if you like. I'm not interested in Paul Morgan, either. I merely went out with him last night because I knew you have been boasting about hooking him, and after the way you spread that talk yesterday, I felt that you deserved a let-down.'

'Why don't you just do your job and leave it at that?' suggested Della.

They worked in silence until Sister Wade appeared and called Della away. The girl had hardly departed before Vince Braddock sneaked into the kitchen, startling Lynn, who was musing over the events of the previous day as she continued with her work.

'You made me jump!' she complained, when Vince suddenly appeared at her side.

'You're a nice one!' he snapped. 'Fancy letting me down like that!'

Lynn gazed at him with wondering eyes. 'What are you talking about?' she demanded.

'I've been asking you for weeks to go out with me, but you've sworn off men, so you said. Then I come on duty this morning, and I hear Paul Morgan spent the evening with you.'

Sister Wade looked into the kitchen at that moment, and Vince backed away, his expression filled with confusion. Lynn smiled as he departed, and Sister Wade came to her side.

'Something wrong, Sister?' asked Lynn, looking into her superior's serene brown eyes.

'No. For the first time, I think I can say that I'm fairly certain that everything will run smoothly around here. During the time you've been in the wilderness since your broken romance, this hospital hasn't been a safe place in which to work, but now you're seeing Doctor Morgan, we should be able to get back to normal.'

'I saw him last night, but that doesn't mean I'm going to see him again,' Lynn said. 'What gave you that idea, Sister?'

'There could be something in that. If Doctor Morgan can put up with you for more than one evening, then he's an even better man than I think he is.'

Lynn smiled and splashed her superior with some soapy water, and Sister Wade departed, pausing in the doorway to give some instructions.

'You're almost done in here, Nurse. When the place is tidy, would you check out the linen cupboard? Carry out a complete inventory.'

'Very well, Sister.' Lynn had the feeling that she was being deliberately kept out of the wards, but she pushed the thought aside because she knew Sister Wade was extremely fair.

She paused in the doorway to look around the kitchen when she had finished cleaning, and nodded approvingly. There wasn't a thing out of place and it really was spotless. She was almost tempted to fetch Sister Wade to get her superior to check upon her handiwork, work, but when she glanced along the corridor, she saw the Sister in the ward with Paul, making a round of the patients. She studied Paul for a moment, recalling the events of the previous evening, and there was a smile on her lips as she went to the big linen cupboard, armed with a pen and pad.

She had to use a ladder to get to the top shelf of the big cupboard, and soon became absorbed in the task of checking the number of articles on the shelves. But her subconscious mind was fixed on Paul Morgan, and she could recall all too easily the way his eyes twinkled when he smiled and how a dimple formed in his chin at times. When she realised the slant her thoughts were taking she shook her head and forced herself to concentrate upon her work.

'Nurse, stop that day-dreaming and come here,' snapped Sister Wade, causing Lynn to almost fall off the ladder in surprise.

Lynn descended and turned to face a wrathful superior, and a frown touched her forehead as she gauged the degree of passion in Sister Wade's mind.

'What are you doing, Nurse?'

'Checking the linen cupboard, as you instructed, Sister.'

'But didn't I tell you to finish cleaning the kitchen first? Matron will be around in a few minutes, and that kitchen looks like a pigsty. You couldn't have made it look worse unless you had deliberately tried in order to cause trouble for me. I've put two juniors in there to put it right.'

'But I left it looking like a new pin!' protested Lynn, turning to go to the kitchen.

'Stay here!' snapped her superior. 'I want you to keep out of it. The place has been deliberately dirtied. It was cleaner when I looked in on you some minutes ago, so don't try to deny anything. I'm getting tired of this business. A hospital is no place for irresponsibility. If Matron does appear before the mess is put right, then I'll tell her exactly why it was in that condition and let her deal with you.'

Lynn opened her mouth to protest, but closed it when she saw Paul standing behind Sister Wade, and he was shaking his head slightly, warning her to remain silent. She clenched her teeth. The phantom joker had apparently struck again, and she was left holding the can, as usual.

'Sister,' interrupted Paul, 'I looked into the kitchen just before we started our round and Nurse Avery had the place looking spick and span. You said it was clean when you looked in upon her. I'm certain, from what I've seen around the hospital, that one of the nursing staff has a grudge against Nurse Avery, and she is taking every opportunity to cause trouble for her.'

'Are you telling me that one of my nurses deliberately went into that kitchen and messed it up just to get Nurse Avery into trouble, Doctor?' demanded Sister Wade.

'That's how it seems to me,' he retorted.

'Well, I look at it from the opposite angle, Doctor. This is not the first time Nurse Avery has been involved in something of this nature, and she has been warned that if these occurrences don't cease then she will be in hot water; very hot water.'

'I'll tell you just once, Sister, that I left the kitchen looking like a new pin,' snapped Lynn, angered by the situation. 'If you can't accept that, then you must really think I am the most irresponsible nurse in the hospital. Well, I'm tired of taking the blame for things I don't do. If you like, I'll see Matron as soon as possible and quit the job. I don't have to tolerate this sort of business! I do my best, and I'm a good nurse. I'm needed here because there is a shortage of trained nurses, but if I'm going to be kept doing the menial tasks, which are the work of juniors, then I might as well leave and let you all get on with it. That's all I have to say upon the subject. Now what is it you want me to do now? Shall I go and clean out the toilets?'

She lapsed into silence, her face flushed, her blue eyes sparkling, and she clenched her teeth as she awaited her superior's reply. She knew she ought to have kept quiet, but her sense of justice was offended and she seethed with anger.

Before Sister Wade could make any

reply to Lynn's outburst, they heard the sound of firm footsteps in the corridor, and turned as one to glance along its length. Lynn frowned when she saw Matron approaching, and a determined look came to her face. She would rather resign her position than accept responsibility for something she hadn't done. Her mind was made up about that. But Paul uttered an unintelligible sound and glanced at Sister Wade.

'I'll keep her talking for a few minutes,' he said, and went striding along the corridor towards Matron. 'Good morning, Matron,' he greeted her loudly. 'I've been keeping an eye open for you. May I interrupt your rounds for a few moments? There's a matter I'd like to discuss with you.'

'Certainly, Doctor. There's nothing wrong, I hope!' Matron glanced along the corridor. 'Shall we use Sister Wade's office?'

Lynn sighed heavily as Paul escorted Matron into the office, then looked into

Sister Wade's flushed face. Her superior was shaking her head slowly, but there was uncertainty in her eyes now.

'I don't know what to make of this, Nurse,' she said slowly. 'I can't really believe that you would deliberately do such things. They're completely out of character for you, and yet they do occur, and I can't accept that any responsible nurse would go out of her way to cause trouble for you.'

'But you think I would do it to cause trouble for someone else,' snapped Lynn. 'If that is the case, then I'm quite prepared to leave, Sister. I can't continue working under such intolerable conditions. Either I'm trusted as all the other nurses, or I'll see Matron myself and quit.'

'I've always kept an open mind about you,' said Sister Wade uncertainly. 'If you are telling the truth, then someone is acting in an extremely unprofessional manner and I would like to find out who it is.'

'I think I can tell you, but I won't

mention any names because I don't have the proof.'

'Very well, let's leave this for a moment. It's obvious that you have a strong ally in Doctor Morgan, and that kitchen was certainly looking quite clean when I last looked in on you. I'll try to find out where all the members of the staff were between the time you left it and I discovered the state it was in. Don't say anything to anyone about it and I'll do some investigating. Meanwhile, you can go on the ward and take charge of the children who are out of bed. Send Nurse Tate to me. I'll be in the kitchen.'

Lynn forced herself to assume a calm expression as she entered the ward and faced Della, who was attending to the children not confined to their beds. 'Hello, Della,' she said quite cheerfully, although it was an effort to maintain such a friendly attitude. 'I'm to take over from you. Sister Wade wants to see you. She said she would be in the kitchen.'

Della averted her gaze and departed immediately, and Lynn turned her attention to the children. There were several small groups of youngsters — one group at the table playing games, another sitting on the floor and playing with toys, and three boys, one wearing leg irons, playing tag around the table. She fought down her outraged feelings and concentrated upon the children, and her anger slowly subsided.

Matron came into the ward some minutes later, and spoke cheerfully to her. Sister Wade appeared, coming to Matron's side, and apologised for not being on hand upon Matron's arrival. She glanced at Lynn, but her expression conveyed nothing.

'Nurse, perhaps you'd finish that job of checking the linen now,' she instructed.

'Yes, Sister.' Lynn suppressed a sigh and left the ward again, and when she reached the linen cupboard, she found Paul waiting there.

'Hello,' he said gravely. 'Have you got that little problem sorted out?'

'I doubt it,' she replied, glancing back towards the ward. 'And I'd better set to work or I'll be in more trouble.'

'You were not to blame for that. Sister Wade knows it. I'm sure she'll find out who was responsible, and then we can put an end of this persecution you're suffering.'

'It doesn't matter.' She sighed heavily. 'I'm getting tired of it. I'm really beginning to think of quitting.'

'You don't strike me as being a quitter,' he said quietly and she felt a warm glow of pleasure at the note in his voice.

'I'd just like to find out who is responsible,' she retorted, then sighed. 'But it doesn't matter. In future, I'll ensure that there's always a witness around when I'm doing something, and get Sister to check me out afterwards. Now I'm on my guard, I'll find out what's going on.'

'I wanted to thank you for a most

pleasant evening,' he said.

'I'm glad you enjoyed yourself. No doubt you'll avail yourself of my father's open invitation.'

'I'd like to, but I don't want to intrude or impose. You didn't seem very happy with my presence last night.'

'Really?' She permitted surprise to reveal itself in her expression. 'What on earth gave you that idea?'

He smiled, but Lynn was serious, and she studied him closely. He shrugged, shaking his head.

'I rather pushed myself on to you yesterday, asking you out in front of one of the nurses. You practically had to say 'yes', didn't you?'

'I certainly didn't. Just ask Vince Braddock. I've turned him down times without number in front of other people.'

'But he expects to get turned down. He asks just about every nurse on the staff for a date. I have never done that. I thought you accepted merely because you wanted to spite Nurse Tate.'

Lynn smiled. 'You mustn't take too much notice of what I say sometimes. I'm merely covering up my real feelings.'

'Then would I be imposing if I came out to your home this evening?'

'I don't think so. Just drive up and come around to the stable. I shall be there. I don't know about my parents though.'

The rest of the day passed without incident, and Lynn did not realise until after lunch that Della was no longer around. When she noticed that her colleague was not on duty, she sought out Gwen and asked about Della.

'Sister Wade transferred her to Men's Surgical,' said Gwen, 'and a good job, too. I think she messed up the kitchen after you'd finished cleaning it. I saw her leave the ward for a few moments about that time. But I couldn't swear to it that the kitchen was her objective. I ought to have watched her, knowing what she is. But you had a go at Sister Wade, didn't you?'

'I lost my temper, which was unfortunate,' said Lynn ruefully. 'But I think it cleared the air. However, I'm ready to quit my job if this business of blaming me for everything that goes wrong doesn't stop, and I made that clear.'

'Good for you.' Gwen glanced around. 'You know, Lynn, I admire you for the way you stand up to everyone. You even had a go at Doctor Morgan.'

'I will, if I'm in the right,' retorted Lynn. 'But Della won't like being moved out of here on account of me, will she?'

'She can't do anything about you now, can she?' Gwen smiled warmly. 'I'd rather have you working here than Della.'

'Perhaps you'd put that in writing,' suggested Lynn. 'I could do with some references.'

Sister Wade approached, and Gwen departed hastily to continue her work. Lynn eyed her superior.

'Nurse, prepare that cubicle we keep

for emergencies, will you? And then clean the balcony. It's getting warm enough these afternoons to get some of the children out there in the sunshine.'

'Have we got a new admission coming in?' asked Lynn.

'Yes. She's pretty seriously ill, too! Doctor Morgan doesn't hold out much hope for her survival. She's been badly neglected. Her parents are in prison awaiting criminal charges.'

Lynn frowned as she went to carry out her instructions, and wondered how parents could possibly fall into such a state as to neglect children. They had to be sick, she surmised, and told herself that they were not really to blame for their actions. But that didn't help the children involved, and her thoughts were sombre.

But she looked forward to getting the children out on to the balcony, which faced south and was always used in summer-time for the children. The big glass doors were opened and Lynn had a junior nurse to help her prepare the area. In the summer, there were always less children suffering illness and more who came in for simple surgery — tonsils and other minor operations. Consequently, the wards were usually filled with children recovering from such operations, and they were a lively lot as they went through the stages of convalescence.

Lynn found the time passing quickly, and went off duty, at six, her mind filled with many impressions which needed to be considered. She had seen the neglected child when she had been admitted, and was disturbed by the sight of the thin, half-starved body, the frightened expression upon sickly face. Tina was almost four years old, and seemed scarcely the size of a child aged two. There were dark bruises on her body, and Lynn heard Paul mutter angrily under his breath as the child had cringed from him when he examined her.

When he arrived at the house just after seven, he was still angry, and Lynn was surprised by his concern. He had always been objective in his dealings with patients. It was the only attitude that succeeded. One did everything possible for a patient, but if that patient died then one turned away to care for the next.

'I'd like to horsewhip that father,' he snapped.

'Come on, Paul,' she replied. 'You know as well as I do that such people must be sick to treat children that way.'

'Some are, and some are just plain sadists. This one is the child's stepfather, and it seems he told the police that he ill-treated her because she was not his child.'

'And the mother?'

'She's so besotted with the man that she said nothing when he ill-treated the child. She must be half-witted, completely lacking in mother-instinct.'

'You surprise me!' Lynn looked at him, with wonder in her blue eyes. 'So you do have a heart after all!'

'What's that supposed to mean?' he

countered angrily. 'Don't tell me you weren't moved by the sight of that child.'

'I was, and I'm in a mood now because of her, but I feel a sense of hopelessness because of it. Those two who call themselves parents can only be sick to treat a child in that manner. But how do you start to treat people like that?'

Lynn shook her head as she regarded him. It was the first time she had seen him really aroused by any issue, and he smiled ruefully as he met her gaze. 'Perhaps I shouldn't have come here this evening, feeling the way I do,' he admitted. 'But I had to get away from all that. It was quite a day, wasn't it?'

'Mine wasn't so bad after I cleared the air this morning.' Lynn suppressed a sigh. 'Come on, let's take a ride, shall we?'

He nodded and they went around to the stables.

'Father said that if you came this evening, perhaps you'd give Captain a run. He's the sorrel. But be careful with him, Paul. He's prone to bucking a bit at odd moments, and if you're not warned he could take you by surprise and unseat you, and if he takes hold of the bit you'll never stop him. He's bolted with Father several times.'

'I like a challenge,' he retorted, and went to saddle the sorrel.

Lynn saddled her chestnut and led the mare outside. She mounted and waited for Paul to appear, and smiled when he mounted swiftly and then fought for control as Captain went through his usual routine of bucking and kicking. After a few moments, Captain realised that he had a master on his back and settled down.

Paul was still angry over the neglected child and said little as they cantered along the path, side by side. While he was lost in his thoughts, she studied him, trying to pinpoint exactly what it was about him that attracted her. She liked the line of his jaw and the way his brows curved above those keen brown eyes. But there were more intangible attractions, and they seemed to have greater power than any physical attribute.

'Are you trying to memorise what I look like?' he demanded suddenly, and Lynn realised that he had noticed she was staring at him.

'I know what you look like,' she retorted in her old, waspish manner. 'I was just wondering what makes you tick.'

He smiled. 'I'm plain enough to analyse,' he said. 'You are the one who is complex.'

'I like that!' She tried to sound offended, but there was a smile on her lips. 'Are you trying to pick a fight with me?'

'Certainly not. But that wouldn't be a hard thing to do, the way you're always prepared to attack.'

'My reputation again.' She sighed. 'In reality, I like the quiet life, but nobody seems to believe that.'

He pushed the sorrel into a gallop,

and immediately found the animal bucking and kicking. Lynn reined up, watching anxiously, but Paul had been alert and soon brought the horse under control. His exertions seemed to take some of the misery out of his mind, for he grinned in his normal way, and suddenly Lynn felt closer to him as instinctive understanding flowed through her. She felt that she had his character pinpointed now, and there was a marked gentleness in her voice when she spoke to him.

'You can certainly handle a horse,' she complimented. 'My father was the best horseman I've ever seen, but I don't think he could have sat tight as you did.'

'There's many a slip,' said Paul, smiling, and his tone was warm. 'Come on. We're wasting time. It will soon be dark. I've waited all day for this, and I don't think I shall be free tomorrow evening. Let's make the most of it.'

Lynn nodded, and rode at his side, but she found herself thinking that he really was only interested in coming to the place for the opportunity to ride the horses, and the thought depressed her. Despite her determination otherwise, she was already wishing that their relationship was on a more personal footing.

They stabled the horses as dusk was falling. She could feel an urge rising inside her that was increasing with intensity, and there was no real desire in her mind to fight against it. She wanted Paul to show an interest in her, there was no denying the fact.

'I think I'll be getting home,' he said, cutting across her thoughts as they left the stable. 'I have some reading to catch up on. Apart from that, I don't want to overstay my welcome. Your parents won't like it if I show my face in your home every evening of the week.'

'My parents aren't at home, and the least you could do in return for the pleasure you're received, is to accept my invitation to come in for a drink.'

'I didn't know you were going to

invite me,' he said. 'Fine. I'll come in for a few minutes.'

'Don't bother, if you think it will be a bit of a strain,' she retorted flippantly.

'Still the same old Lynn Avery!' he commented, as they walked through the shadows towards the house, and for a moment their shoulders brushed.

Lynn caught her breath, fighting the impulse to turn towards him, wanting him to take her into his arms, and she was thankful for the gloom because it concealed her features. She was shaken by the swiftly changing attitude that had overtaken her. Two days ago, she had been perfectly happy on her own. Now he had stepped into her life and she was on the edge of the precipice again. But he had no interest in her, and was making that perfectly clear.

They entered the house and she led the way into the lounge and took her time pouring him a drink. He sat in one of the big easy chairs in front of the fireplace, and she wished he had chosen the sofa so that she could have joined him.

'Thank you, Lynn,' he said, as he accepted the drink, and she turned to occupy the other easy chair.

'Be careful that I haven't put something in it,' she warned darkly.

'Why would you do that?' he asked. 'I suppose you think I'm taking you for granted, or just using you as a means to get some enjoyment from life. Perhaps I ought to ask you to go out for an evening, and when I say out I mean out. Would you dress up and go to a smart restaurant or to the theatre with me?'

Lynn's heart seemed to lurch at his words, but she forced a smile. It was nice of him, but she wasn't going to accept an evening out as payment for the horse-riding he so obviously enjoyed and only came for. 'You know what I said about detesting the social round. I think I much prefer to remain around here when I'm off duty. It enables me to relax that much more.

You don't have to go out of your way to be nice to me. Be thankful that you have the opportunity to come and go as you please.'

'Just as you like.' He nodded, draining his glass and getting to his feet. 'Now I think I really ought to be going.'

'Sorry I dragged you in,' she said, 'but I wouldn't want to be accused of being anti-social.'

'You're the perfect hostess. You insult your guests as you please, and you're charming with it.'

'It's different to the usual run of hypocrites, who make you feel welcome and talk about you behind your back.'

'True. Well, I'll see you tomorrow, Lynn.' He started towards the door and Lynn followed him, wishing she could think of some excuse to delay him, but he opened the front door and stepped outside, barely turning to wish her good night before moving off into the night to his car.

A sigh escaped Lynn as she closed

the door after his departure, and she felt unsettled as she went back to the lounge. The time was barely nine o'clock, and it was too early for her to go to bed.

Making an impetuous decision, she went up to her room and changed into a skirt and blouse, then went to find Mrs. Moss, who was watching her portable TV set in her room.

'If Mother should come in and ask for me, tell her I've gone out to see some of the nurses from the hospital,' said Lynn.

'You're going out?' demanded Mrs. Moss, in some surprise. 'Whatever is this world coming to? Where's the good doctor? Are you going with him?'

'No, I'm not! He's gone home. He only comes here to ride the horses. I'm ready for bed, actually, but it's far too early, and if I go to bed now, I'll be awake early in the morning, so I thought I'd have a run into town. I won't be more than an hour.'

'I'll tell your mother if she should

ask.' Mrs. Moss nodded and returned to the small screen.

Lynn picked up her handbag and went out to her car, intent upon visiting the local where the nursing fraternity usually met when off duty. It was around the corner from the hospital, and Lynn had not been there since the early days of her romance with Robert.

She drove into the town centre and left the car in a multi-storey car park, then went to the little pub, pausing outside in the shadows, listening to the sounds emanating from its interior. A sudden bout of diffidence overwhelmed her for it would be like stepping back into the past, except that some of the familiar faces would no longer be present. But she was not afraid of the past, she reasoned, and took a deep breath and pushed open the door.

The big, familiar room looked as if it hadn't changed in the past five years, and she paused to glance around. It was fairly well crowded, and there were a number of her colleagues present. One of the first people she saw was Della Tate, and the girl took a second look at her, surprise showing in her face at sight of Lynn. But there were closer friends of Lynn's present, and Chrissie Wright was seated in a corner — their old, favourite seat when they had been student nurses, and Chrissie caught sight of her and came across. Her expression showing great delight.

'Lynn, how lovely seeing you here! Is anything wrong?'

'No.' Lynn smiled. 'I was passing, and when I heard the voices in here, it reminded me of the old days, so I thought I'd look in and see if it had changed at all.'

'It hasn't changed a bit.' Chrissie took hold of her arm and began to lead her towards the corner. 'If you look at some of those pies on the counter, you'll see that they're the same ones you used to joke about. What will you drink?'

'Let me buy the drinks,' pleaded Lynn. 'This is my visit and I'll do the honours.' She glanced at the other three nurses at the table one of whom was Gwen Barber, who smiled and lifted an acknowledging hand.

Lynn bought a round of drinks and sat down at the table. As she gazed around, her mind dipped into the past and she recalled some painful memories. But she also realised that she had been cutting herself off from reality. The world had continued turning while she had been moping at home. Paul had seen that, and perhaps it was why he had offered to take her out one evening. She made a mental note to accept his offer if he made it again.

'Vince Braddock was in a short time ago,' said Chrissie. 'He's on duty this evening, but he usually pops in to look over the field. If he saw you he'd turn somersaults, Lynn. He's always asking why you never show up around here.'

'I feel sorry for Vince,' replied Lynn, smiling. 'It's nothing personal, but he's too like Robert for me. They might have stepped out of the same mould.'

'Strange you should say that, but I've noticed it, too,' said Chrissie. 'But how did you happen to be passing, Lynn? I heard that Doctor Morgan was going out to your place this evening.'

'He was out there,' admitted Lynn.

'And you let him get away?' demanded Gwen, shaking her head. 'You said you only accepted his date to put a spoke in Della's wheel, but I didn't think you really meant it. No girl in her right mind would pass up Paul Morgan.'

'Well, I have,' Lynn said decisively. 'He comes out to ride Father's horses, and he did ask me to spend an evening with him, but I turned him down.'

'There's no justice in this world,' observed Gwen sadly. 'I know a dozen nurses who would give almost anything to spend an evening in his company and you have to turn him down!'

The rest of the evening passed quickly, and Lynn was thankful. She refused all further offers of a drink, and, just before she began to think of leaving, the lounge door was opened and Vince Braddock entered. He glanced casually around the big room, and did a kind of double-take when he saw Lynn at the corner table. His expression changed immediately and he came across.

'Look at the wolf at work,' whispered Chrissie, and Lynn chuckled.

'What on earth are you doing here?' demanded Vince.

'You said that as if I have no right to be here,' countered Lynn.

'Where's Morgan?' Vince glanced around quickly. 'Did he bring you in?'

'No, he didn't. I'm quite capable of finding this place by myself.'

'Then I'll see you home. I'm on my break right now.'

'Sorry. I've got my car in the multi-storey. I came alone and I'll go home the same way.' Lynn smiled as she arose, glancing around at her friends. 'It was nice coming in here again,' she commented. 'I think we'll have to get together more often.'

'I've always said the place was never the same without you,' said Chrissie. 'See you at the hospital tomorrow, Lynn.'

'Good night!' Lynn turned to the door and Vince went with her, opening the door for her.

'I'll see you to your car,' he said, and she glanced at him with a frown.

'That's all right. I know where I left it.'

'That multi-storey car park isn't a nice place to be at this time of the night,' he said firmly. 'There's a tough bunch who hang around it and you could find trouble. People have been mugged in there, Lynn.'

'I accept your protection,' she answered in resignation, and they walked along the street to the car park.

'Lynn, I'm glad you decided to come out this evening because I've been wanting to talk to you for some time now and never found the right opportunity. You've always got some excuse for not seeing me, and I've reached the point where I've got to compel you to listen.'

Lynn stifled a sigh, for she could guess what was in his mind, and she felt sorry for him.

'I've never made excuses for not seeing you,' she replied quietly. 'I've always told you the truth. I don't want to go out with you, Vince. It's nothing personal. I value you as a friend. We've known each other for a long time.'

'That's the point. I don't want to be merely a friend. I seem to remember that before you started going around with Robert, we got together several times. Now that Robert has gone out of your life and you've got over it, I think it would do you good to get out and about again, to mix with people once more. I've seen it in your face. You need company, Lynn, and don't try to deny it, because you know I'm speaking the truth.'

'Perhaps you are, in that respect,' she replied, as they mounted the stairs to the floor where she had parked her car.

'But I think I've made my attitude towards you very plain, Vince, and I don't want to have to say hurtful things to really put you off. I realised before I met Robert that you and I were not meant for each other, and that's why I stopped seeing you. Why don't you find yourself a nice girl instead of making a reputation for yourself by chasing every nurse on the staff?'

'That's the reputation I've gained,' he said sadly. 'But I only go around with the others because I'm lonely and can't have you. I love you, Lynn, and have always loved you. But you're inaccessible! There's a barrier as high as the Himalayas between us.'

He paused, clasping her elbow, and the light from a near-by lamp fell full upon his harshly-set features, revealing misery in every line of his countenance. She had never seen him in anything but a cheerful mood, and this change shook her.

'You know what it's like to have a reputation that you don't deserve,' he said in a low-pitched voice. 'Why don't you give me a chance, Lynn? We might be able to make a go of it. You could change your ideas about me.'

'I'm sorry, but I think it would only complicate our lives. I've experienced one unhappy affair and I'm not prepared to let myself in for another entanglement.'

'What about Morgan? You're seeing him.' There was resentment in Vince's voice, and Lynn shook herself free of his arm and walked on up the steps.

'I don't want to discuss him, Vince. That has nothing to do with you. But I will tell you that I'm not going out with him. He's coming to our place to help exercise my father's horses.'

He gazed at her from under lowering brows, and a sigh escaped him. 'I know the fact that I'm in love with you doesn't give me any right to intrude into your affairs, but I wouldn't want to see you get hurt again, Lynn. I don't know why, but I have the feeling that you could be in for trouble with

Morgan if you start getting interested in him. There's something about him that doesn't quite ring true.'

'I don't know what you mean, and I have no desire to hear more.' Lynn paused and faced him. 'Now you'd better get back to the hospital. My car is over there and I can reach it quite safely from here.'

'The least you can do is drop me off at the gates,' he said. 'Or are you afraid to be seen with me?'

'Don't be silly,' she retorted. 'Come and get into the car, for heaven's sake.'

She drove out of the park and went round the block to approach the hospital, and when she pulled up at the kerb by the main gate, she kept the engine running.

'Lynn,' he said, turning towards her.

'Vince, don't say anything more,' she cut in. 'You can only make matters worse.'

He gazed at her in silence for a moment, then shook his head, and she heard him exhale sharply. The next moment, he leaned towards her, and, before she realised what he was about to do, had gathered her in his powerful arms and was kissing her passionately. Lynn was so surprised by his action that she could not resist for several seconds, and his mouth bruised her lips. Then she pushed him away.

She slapped his face hard, stinging her right hand. He jerked back from her, his face a pale blur in the shadows, and the silence that descended between them was heavy, throbbing with tension.

'You've just ended a fine friendship, Vince,' she said sharply. 'Don't ever come near me again, on duty or off duty, do you understand?'

'What are you made of?' he asked. 'Are you the Ice Queen? I'm crazy about you, Lynn, and I'm getting desperate because I think you're falling in love with Paul Morgan. I've got to make an attempt to win you now or I'll never manage it.'

'You never had a chance of getting

me serious about you,' she answered. 'I'm sorry, Vince, but that's the way it is. And after this little episode, I think it would be better if you stayed out of my way. I shall certainly avoid you in future.'

He gazed at her, his face shadowed, but she could see the set of his strong jaw. He sighed heavily and shook his head, then jerked open the car door and got out.

For a moment, she sat considering Vince, aware of what he must be suffering, and then she thought of Paul and the awakening emotions for him in her breast. Against her wishes, she was falling in love with him, and it was a bitter-sweet sensation. She could sympathise with Vince, but there was no way she could help him, and all she could do was hope that he would get over it.

4

Lynn went on duty next morning in a strange mood, unable to pinpoint exactly what was worrying her, gnawing at her subconscious mind. The incident she'd had with Vince had not helped her at all, but the real problem seemed to be her feelings for Paul and his apparent lack of interest in her.

But duty forced all personal problems aside, and she went into Children's and found Sister Wade already in the ward and supervising the usual round of work. Lynn was extremely popular with all the children, and they greeted her like a long-lost friend returning after an absence of years.

Sister Wade called her across to where Paul was examining little Betty Rayner, who had fallen off a swing and had suffered concussion and a badly gashed head.

'Take Betty to the dressing cubicle,' directed Sister Wade. 'Her stitches can come out this morning. I'll be along to take them out myself.'

'Yes, Sister.' Lynn looked into the small blonde girl's blue eyes and saw fear in them. She had recovered from her concussion and the bandage which had been around her head for a week had been removed. 'Come along, Betty,' said Lynn as Sister Wade turned away. 'Let's put on your dressing-gown, shall we?'

'Will it hurt, Nurse?' the youngster demanded doubtfully, and there was a hint of tears in her wide eyes.

'No, dear.' Lynn smiled reassuringly as she helped the youngster into her dressing-gown. 'You're almost better now, and you can sit on my lap while Sister Wade attends to you. Sister Wade wouldn't hurt you. We all love you.'

'It hurt when I came in,' retorted the child.

'You were very badly hurt then, but now you've got better. I promise that you won't feel anything.' Lynn carried the girl along the ward to the cubicle, and Betty clung to her when Sister Wade entered. Lynn kissed the child's forehead, and Sister Wade nodded approvingly.

'Well, Betty,' she said softly. 'So you're better at last. Your mummy has been called and she's coming this morning to take you home. But first I have to take those stitches out, so you just sit quite still and Nurse Avery will hold you. It won't hurt, so don't be afraid.'

The child twisted her fingers in the material of Lynn's uniform, and Lynn held her close. Sister Wade worked quickly but gently, and there was no sound from their small patient. Lynn saw that Betty had closed her eyes, and she glanced over the child's head at Sister Wade, who gave a faint smile.

'There you are, Betty,' she said at length. 'That didn't hurt, did it?'

'Are they out?' demanded the child, opening her eyes.

'Yes. Now Nurse Avery will take you back to your bed, and I want you to remain there quietly until your mummy comes for you. She telephoned to say that she would be here very soon.'

Lynn took the child back to her bed, and, after putting her in it, returned to her duties, hearing Betty proudly reporting to her neighbour that she hadn't felt the stitches coming out. She smiled in relief and came face to face with Paul.

'Good morning,' she said, glancing around to see Sister Wade entering the ward.

'Good morning,' he responded, and she frowned a little as she glanced at his set features. 'I'd like to talk to you when we get a free moment.'

'My lunch break begins at twelve-thirty,' she responded. 'Is something wrong?'

'No, of course not. Perhaps I can see you this evening.'

'Certainly. I'm off every night this week. Next week, I'll be on the two till ten shift. Will you be coming out to our place this evening?'

'Yes, I'd like to. It's obvious I'm not going to get you to go out around the town with me.' He nodded and went on his way, glancing back at her with his incisive gaze. 'I'll see you later,' he added.

Lynn frowned as she gazed after him, for she knew then that something was wrong although he had denied having problems. Then it struck her that he might have heard about her going out after he had left her the previous evening. Someone was certain to tell him, and she had not considered that. She sighed, and Sister Wade paused at her side.

'Day-dreaming, Nurse, or don't you have anything to do?' she queried.

'Sorry, Sister.' Lynn jerked her mind back to duty, and when she was in the kitchen with Gwen, preparing lunch for the patients, she found the opportunity to broach the subject of the previous evening.

'It was nice seeing you there last night, Lynn,' observed her colleague. 'Perhaps you'll come again now. The place hasn't really been the same without you. But what about Vince? It was a pity he showed up. When I saw him, I knew you wouldn't be able to get away from him.'

'I don't think he'll bother me again,' said Lynn.

'Surely you didn't have a fight with him!'

'No. But I let him know exactly where he stood with me.'

When she went off duty for lunch, she went out to her car in the park, hoping to see Paul there, but there was no sign of him and she went into the dining-room for her meal, afterwards returning to the car park to see Paul. But he did not show up and she went back on duty filled with a gnawing urgency as her imagination ran riot. The afternoon seemed long, despite the fact that she and the other nurses were kept busy. The hospital rules were that Children's Ward was open to visitors all the time, and there was always some mother wanting information about the progress of one or another of the youngsters, or the patients themselves wanted to introduce the nurses to their parents. But, eventually, Lynn departed from the hospital and drove homewards, feeling unusually weary, and after tea she sat in the kitchen talking to Mrs. Moss.

'You're looking tired, Lynn,' remarked the housekeeper.

'I feel it. Are Mother and Father coming home this evening?'

'Your mother telephoned to say they wouldn't be home. Are you going out?'

'No, I'm far too tired. I don't think I'll even go riding this evening.'

'Is Doctor Morgan coming over?'

'Yes. He can ride if he wishes. I'm going to relax in the lounge. I'll answer the door if the bell rings, Mrs. Moss, because it will only be Doctor Morgan.'

'Only!' The housekeeper smiled. 'You don't have to tell me, Lynn. I can see that you're interested in him.'

'I won't argue with you. But everyone is reading some kind of significance into my association with Paul. It will die a natural death, I presume.'

She went into the lounge and settled back with the newspaper, but her mind was not relaxed and she barely read the news, her thoughts turning over and over on the events and impressions of the day. Something was worrying Paul and she was concerned. Then the doorbell rang and she sprang up and rushed to the door, barely able to control herself before entering the hall and moving slowly to answer. When she opened the door, she found Paul standing there, and her spirits seemed to waver when she noted the tense lines around his mouth.

'Hello,' she said brightly. 'I'd only just sat down. For some unknown reason, I feel more tired than usual.'

'Perhaps that's because you went out

last night after I left,' he said coolly.

'Yes, I went out. Is there a law against it?' She hadn't meant to snap at him.

'Of course not.' His hard expression did not change. 'You're perfectly free to do exactly what you like, but I had asked you to go out with me and you declined on the grounds that you preferred the rustic life and didn't like the high spots. Yet as soon as I leave here you're out with Vince Braddock. He wasted no time rubbing it in this morning.'

'Did he?' Lynn's eyes were narrowed and gleaming as she studied his intent face. 'I expect he exaggerated, as usual. I'll wager that he didn't tell you the nature of the conversation I had with him.'

'I'm not interested in that,' he retorted.

'Then why are you upset?'

'Who said I was upset?'

'Nobody has to say so. It's patently obvious.' Lynn could not control the sharpness of her tones. 'Are you coming in or did you come merely to ride? If it's the riding, then you know where the stables are. Or would you like me to come and saddle a horse for you?'

For a moment, there was a heavy silence, and Lynn glared at him, breathing harshly. His unblinking gaze seemed to cut right through her, and then he shook his head.

'Are your parents at home?' he asked.

'No, they won't be in until late.'

'All right. I'll take one of the horses out to exercise. Are you riding this evening?'

'No, I'm too tired.'

'Sorry I dragged you out of your chair,' he commented. 'I'll go round to the stable.'

He stepped back and moved away and Lynn closed the door, leaning against it in mortification as she considered what had passed between them. She realised that from his point of view, her behaviour must have seemed erratic, but she could not explain it without divulging her feelings for him.

She went to the landing on the stairs and peered out across the fields, spotting Paul in the distance, riding one of the horses, and she had to fight down the impulse to go out to him. He was riding stiffly, and she knew he was angry because she had gone out without his knowledge. But did his attitude mean that he cared for her? She doubted it. Perhaps his pride had been hurt. That seemed more likely.

When he returned the horse to the stable, she expected him to come to the house, and went down to the lounge, but, minutes later, she heard the sound of his car driving away and ran to the window to see him departing. A surge of emotion struck through her and she had to blink tears from her eyes. She knew misery as she turned away from the window. She was in love with him and nothing would change that fact.

She went to bed before her parents came home, not wanting to face them, and spent a restless night, tossing and turning. It was a welcome relief when it was time to arise and prepare for duty. Yet there was no pleasure in her when she went to the hospital, and she parked her car and strode into the corridors, her eyes narrowed and her expression taut.

Chrissie Wright looked as if she was waiting for Lynn, who paused before her friend and forced a smile.

'I looked for you last night,' said Chrissie. 'I thought you might have joined us again.'

'It was a once-only effort, I'm afraid,' responded Lynn, forcing lightness into her tones. 'I don't like the bright lights and company.'

'You're turning antisocial, my girl. What you need is to climb out of the rut completely. When are you going to take your holiday?'

'I don't know, and I don't really care.' Lynn walked on along the corridor and Chrissie accompanied her. 'Where are you working today?' she queried.

'With you. It's Gwen's day off. She's going over to night duty.'

Sister Wade was already present, having relieved the night nurse at six, and she motioned for Lynn to remain when she gave instructions to Chrissie.

'Nurse, I don't want any more trouble around the wards,' she said, when Chrissie had gone. 'Nurse Tate is coming back to us because of the changes in staff duties, and I know how things are between you two.'

'Correction, Sister,' retorted Lynn. 'I've never said or done anything to upset Nurse Tate. She's always ready to have a go at me though, and I don't have the remotest idea why.'

'The reason's obvious,' came the prompt reply from her superior. 'She was in love with the man you planned to marry.'

'Well, I didn't marry him, and Della is welcome to him, if she can find him.' Lynn shrugged. She was beginning to think that there was a jinx upon her romantic life. 'Just make sure that our paths don't cross, Sister, and there'll be no problem,' she added.

'Don't worry, I'm going to watch her like a hawk, and you'd better do the same. Strange as it may seem to you, Nurse, I don't want to lose you. I know good nursing material when I see it, and you work very well.'

'You've just made my day,' retorted Lynn, smiling. 'What shall I do now?'

'Go into the wards. The kids love you. I'll keep Della out of the way.'

When it was time for Paul's morning rounds, Lynn kept an eye on the door. She spotted Della along the corridor, moving out of and then back into the kitchen, and her blue eyes sparkled as she imagined the girl with her hands in washing-up water.

Then she saw Paul walking along the corridor towards the Sister's office, and as he passed the kitchen door, he paused and glanced inside. Lynn frowned for Della suddenly appeared in the doorway, confronting him, and it was obvious that she had called to him.

Lynn watched, noted that a brief exchange of words passed between them, and then Paul continued towards the Sister's office. But not before Della had gently laid a hand upon his arm. For a brief moment, the girl stood looking up into his face, and then she turned and vanished into the kitchen again.

Paul entered the Sister's office, and Lynn returned to her work, wishing that she had not witnessed the scene. She could not help wondering if Della was the cause for Paul's apparent change of attitude towards her. It was likely, for there were no limits to which Della would not go in order to have her own way.

The day seemed endless, and Lynn realised that it was her attitude, her mental state, which gave her the impression that everything seemed too much. Nothing seemed to go right, and she even fell foul of Sister Wade because her preoccupation caused her to forget an important message which she ought to have passed on.

During lunch, she sat with Chrissie, and heard Della at an adjacent table talking loudly about various members of the staff. There were one or two allusions which might have been directed at Lynn, but she did not rise to the bait, although she noted that Della was glancing in her direction from time to time.

Chrissie seemed to sense that something was amiss, and leaned forward to speak in an undertone. 'What's going on, Lynn? Della has been spreading word around the hospital that you and Doctor Morgan have fallen out.'

'Has she?' Lynn's features set in impassive lines as she regarded her friend's expression of concern. 'Well, how could that be true when there has never been anything between us? I find it quite amusing that everyone should read so much significance into the fact that Paul came out to my home. It had nothing whatever to do with me. He can ride, and my father doesn't have the time to exercise his horses properly, so Paul helps out. I'm afraid everyone is in for a great disappointment if they're expecting lurid developments in a situation which doesn't exist.'

When she and Chrissie were making their way back to the ward, she noticed that Chrissie was glancing at her from time to time.

'What's wrong, Chrissie?' she demanded.

'That's what I was about to ask you,' came the immediate counter. 'You may be able to fool all the others, but I know there is something wrong with you. We've been friends too long, Lynn, for you to pull the wool over my eyes.'

'It must be catching,' persisted Lynn. 'When a rumour goes around, everyone believes it, regardless. What could be wrong?'

'I don't know.' Chrissie shook her head. 'But I do know that you're not your usual self.'

'We all have off-days,' said Lynn. She saw Vince coming along the corridor towards them, and noticed that he seemed miserable. She could sympathise with him, aware of her own misery, which was slowly but surely building up in the back of her mind.

'Hello, Vince,' she greeted him. 'You look as if you have just lost a month's salary.'

He paused, eyeing her nervously.

'If you're thinking of asking me out for the evening then the answer is 'yes',' continued Lynn, and heard a startled gasp from Chrissie, who walked on along the corridor. But Vince showed complete astonishment.

'What on earth has come over you?' he asked. 'I wasn't going to ask you for a date, especially after the other evening. I realise I don't stand any chance with you, so I'm cutting my losses.'

'All right, forget I consented,' she said, and started after Chrissie. But he grasped her arm, and Lynn saw a gleam in his pale eyes.

'Not likely! You said you'd go out

with me and I'm not going to pass that up.' Then he paused. 'There must be a catch to this. Lynn. I've heard a rumour today about trouble between you and Morgan.'

'Really? One of Della's gems, no doubt!' Lynn chuckled. 'I was sitting near her in the dining-room just now and heard her running on. Take no notice of her, Vince. I'll go out with you on the understanding that you don't take it seriously. If you think this is the thin end of the wedge and that we'll go on to better things, then forget about it!'

'I get it.' There was bitterness in his tones. 'You're going to use me to show Morgan that you couldn't care less about him. Are you in love with him, Lynn?'

'Don't be absurd!' she retorted.

'I know what it feels like to be in love with someone who doesn't reciprocate. If that is the situation then going out with me won't help you. You're in for a rough time.'

'Look, do you want to take me out this evening or not?' she demanded.

'Of course I do. I'm off duty. Where would you like to go?'

'Nowhere special! Where you saw me the other evening will do.' Lynn spoke casually. 'I'll come in my car. See you in the car park about seven-thirty.'

With parents visiting all the time in Children's, there were never any quiet periods on the wards, and Lynn found herself working incessantly, happy with the occupation that prevented her thoughts turning inwards. But during the afternoon, she looked up to find Paul in the ward, and he came towards her. Sister Wade was not present, and Lynn glanced around to see if she could retreat before he reached her, but she was at the far end of the ward and had to remain.

'Hello, Lynn,' he greeted her. 'I didn't get the chance to talk to you this morning on my round.'

'I gained the impression that you didn't want to,' she said, speaking before she could even consider her words.

'You're not still put out like you were last night when I came to your home, are you?' he demanded.

'I was not put out last night. What gave you that idea?'

'You wouldn't go riding with me.'

'I was tired last night. I didn't feel like riding. It was nothing personal.'

'Oh, I'm sorry, because I thought there was. But you've been acting strangely for some days now, so I've decided to keep quiet until you get yourself sorted out.'

'Sorted out?' she repeated. 'I don't need sorting out.'

'Well, you're a strange creature if your actions of the past few days have been normal,' he said wryly. With that, he turned away, and Lynn watched him leave the ward, her spirits sinking to zero.

Sister Wade returned to the ward during the afternoon and came to Lynn's side, a quizzical smile in her eyes.

'So you've finally accepted Vince Braddock's invitation to go out,' commented her superior.

'Just for the evening. I'm not treading on your toes, am I, Sister?' Lynn could not prevent the question forming on her lips, and she saw a smile crease Sister Wade's face. 'I don't seem to be able to turn any way without upsetting someone,' she added.

'If I had wanted Vince Braddock, I could have had him a long time ago,' came the surprising reply. 'He's not a bad chap, but not for me, or for the likes of you, Nurse. I say that from the point of view of an interested onlooker. I'm interested because you're working in my ward, and if you find any problems cropping up they may show in your work.'

'You've been listening to the rumours, Sister,' retorted Lynn, smiling faintly, although her eyes remained bright and hard. 'I've been hearing them myself. I don't know what it's all about, but you can rest assured that whatever crops up, my work here won't be affected.'

'I thought you and Doctor Morgan were going to hit it off, but from what I hear, Della Tate has got her wish at last. She's going out with him this evening.'

It was all Lynn could do to maintain an impassive expression at the news, for she was aware that Sister Wade was watching her intently. But evidently her superior was satisfied that the information was no surprise to Lynn, for she nodded and went on:

'Well, so long as the work around here gets done properly, then it doesn't matter to me who goes out with whom. It seems to be the thing these days to chop and change partners. How times change!' She departed, and Lynn returned to her charges on the balcony, her mind filled with miserable speculation.

She went home with little eagerness in her mind for the evening out she had promised to Vince Braddock, and when she entered the large kitchen and found her mother there, she half-wished she could have been alone with her thoughts. But she put on a cheerful expression and forced down her feelings in order to appear natural.

'Hello, Mother,' she said. 'Had a busy day?'

'I'm worn out,' came the reply. 'What about you?'

'It hasn't been too bad. I'm going out this evening.'

'You were out the other evening. That's unusual for you. Who's taking you? Paul?'

'No.' There seemed to be a tugging at Lynn's heart as she replied casually. 'Vince Braddock. You must remember Vince. He came here several times with the crowd I used to go around with before I became serious with Robert.'

'Yes, I remember him. But what about Paul? Mrs. Moss tells me he comes every evening to ride. Will he be coming this evening?'

'I don't think so. I believe he's got a date.'

Mrs. Avery glanced at Lynn, who fancied that her tones had been just a little too casual.

'That seems a strange arrangement after the past few evenings. Has something happened?'

'Happened?' Lynn shook her head. 'I don't know what you mean.'

'I thought you and Paul would naturally drift together. You seemed very well suited to me, and even your father remarked upon the fact.'

'You were probably looking at us with biased gaze,' Lynn said blithely. 'If you're not careful, I'll begin to suspect that you and Father would like to see me married and out of the house.'

'Nonsense! We want to see you do whatever is right for you, and this is your home for as long as you wish to remain, you know that.' Mrs. Avery peered into Lynn's face. 'You don't look very happy, dear,' she accused. 'You can't hide anything from me, you know.'

'There's nothing to hide,' protested

Lynn. She sat down at the table. 'I'd better have some tea and then get ready to go out. I don't want to keep Vince waiting or he'll begin to think that I've stood him up, and he's been asking me for weeks to go out with him.'

Before they finished tea, the kitchen door was opened and her father walked in. He smiled at her, and Lynn arose, wanting to leave before he could begin asking questions. But he kissed her forehead and placed a steady hand on her slim shoulders.

'You can tell Paul, when you see him, that he's worked wonders with my horses. Is he coming out this evening? I'd like to have a chat with him. He told me the other evening that he would like to buy a place around here, and I heard today that old Mrs. Wilkins is thinking of selling up. Now her husband is dead she's planning on moving into a flat nearer the centre of town.'

'But that would make Paul a neighbour,' said Lynn.

'If I didn't know differently, I would

swear that you said it as if you didn't want him to be a neighbour,' her father said with a frown.

'What gave you the idea that I did?' countered Lynn, moving towards the door.

'Have you two had a difference of opinion?' demanded her father, looking at her in startled fashion, then glancing towards Mrs. Avery, who shook her head slightly to warn him into silence.

'No. Paul will still come out here to ride your horses,' said Lynn. 'Now I must hurry. I've got to change, and I'm meeting Vince at the car park in town.'

5

When she drove into the multi-storey car park, Vince was there seated in his car. He alighted, locked his door, and came across to her with a broad smile on his face as she did the same.

'Hello,' he said. 'I was beginning to think you'd had second thoughts. But you're a girl of your word, Lynn. That much I do know about you. Did you hear at the hospital that Morgan is taking Della Tate out this evening?'

'Yes, I heard,' she replied coolly. 'Is that supposed to affect me in some way?'

He pulled a face at her, but remained smiling, and Lynn fancied that he understood how she was feeling. He took her arm as they left the car park and she did not object.

'They'll be surprised in the pub,' remarked Vince, as they crossed the street. 'There's a darts match on this evening. Some of our staff taking on the regulars. It reminds me of the old days, Lynn.'

'The old days hold no magic for me,' she told him.

'You sound like a wet blanket,' he commented. 'I hope I haven't done the wrong thing in getting you out in my company. But knowing me, I wouldn't be surprised if that's the way of it. I never did the right thing in my life.'

'I'm sorry, Vince.' She mellowed immediately. 'I don't want to spoil your evening out. You've waited such a long time for my company, although why you should want it I don't know. I just don't want you to read too much into this outing, that's all.'

They entered the lounge, and already there was a good crowd present, mostly off-duty members of the hospital staff, and the darts team were already practising on the board in the corner. She saw Chrissie and Gwen Barber at a corner table, and fancied that Chrissie looked a bit worried when their glances met and Lynn lifted an acknowledging hand.

Then she looked around more closely to see who was present and her heart almost missed a beat and she fought for self-control.

Seated at a table near the bar were Della and Paul, and when Lynn's eyes met those of Della she saw a mocking expression awaiting her. Paul looked at her keenly, and nodded perceptibly as she let her gaze take in his handsome features. She smiled, but there was a buzzing sound in her ears, and for one awful moment she felt that she might faint from the shock of this meeting.

Then Vince spoke in her ear. 'Didn't you know Della would bring him here this evening?'

'It doesn't matter a whit to me,' she answered. 'I suppose you told Della you would be bringing me here.'

'Of course! I wouldn't want to miss the darts match, would I?'

'Then let's sit at their table,' she

suggested, and saw a shadow of surprise cross Vince's face. 'The place is rather full, isn't it, and will become crowded before very much longer, if I can remember the old days well enough. I told you that I have no social or romantic interest in Paul Morgan, and that's the way it is.'

He nodded reluctantly and led her across to the table by the bar, and it needed all of Lynn's determination to remain impassive. She had to steel herself as pleasantries were exchanged between them, although to her ears they sounded hollow, and she sat down, keenly ware of Paul's presence. But she forced herself to glance around easily, and there was no tremor in her tones as she joined in the conversation that Vince commenced. Yet it seemed to her that, somehow, this had been arranged for her benefit.

When the darts match began, there was a great deal of good-natured bantering, but Lynn felt as if she were apart from everyone, isolated by her attitude towards the situation. She longed for closing time so that she could be set free like a bird from a trap and fly homewards to the sanctuary of her room.

When Vince asked her what she wanted to drink she asked for a pineapple juice, turning a deaf ear to his protests.

'I'm driving myself home, remember,' she said. 'I don't want any alcohol.'

She sat for a long time with the pineapple juice, sipping from it at irregular intervals, and she insisted upon buying Vince a drink. Paul was drinking beer, but had no more than one, and when she offered him a drink, he refused graciously, smiling a little as he met her eyes. But it was an impersonal smile, and she sensed that extra barriers had already gone up in his mind.

Finally, she could stand the atmosphere no longer, and whispered to Vince: 'I'm sorry, Vince, but I can't take any more of this. I have a splitting headache. I think I'd better go home. I'm sorry to spoil your evening, but you have other friends here.'

He began to protest, but she would not be deterred, and he arose and pulled back her chair for her. She took her leave of Paul and Della, aware that the girl was smiling with great satisfaction showing in her expressive features, and when she reached the cold fresh air of the night she paused and took a deep breath.

'The atmosphere in there is so thick you could cut it with a scalpel,' she commented. 'Look, there's no need to see me to my car. Go back to your friends, Vince.'

'Nonsense! I'm not letting you go into that car park alone. Even I look over my shoulder when I go in there after dark. Come on.' He took her arm and led her along the street.

'I'm not used to that kind of entertainment these days,' she apologised.

'Say no more. I can see how it is. Good night, Lynn. Are you sure you're feeling well enough to drive home? I can follow you in my car, if you like.'

'Thanks, but that won't be necessary. Good night, Vince.'

He nodded and stepped back as she got into the car and switched on. He lifted a hand as she backed out and then drove away, and Lynn let her shoulders sag as she left the car park and drove homewards. She really had a headache, and was thankful when she reached home and could go to bed. She lay in the darkness awaiting sleep, but it was a long time coming.

Next morning, she felt better, although there was a sense of sadness in her mind, and as she drove to the hospital she steeled herself for the inevitable cross-examination which would be directed at her by her colleagues. She was determined to give nothing away, and when she met Chrissie in the corridor she greeted her friend with a breeziness she was far from feeling.

'You left early!' accused Chrissie. 'Was something wrong?'

'No. I had a headache, that's all. I'm not used to all that noise, and the cigarette smoke almost choked me.'

But it was easy to forget herself when she confronted her young patients. There had been a new admission during the night, and she found herself at the bedside of a girl of about eight years who lay motionless in her small, white-painted bed, her knees drawn up and her eyes unfocused as she gazed at the near-by wall. She was due for an operation next morning, and seemed bewildered by this big room filled with beds and all the strange children and people around her.

'Hello,' greeted Lynn, smiling in a friendly fashion. 'What's your name?'

The child did not answer, and Lynn pulled her covers straight and placed a hand upon the small forehead. She was a fair-haired girl with blue eyes and long, golden lashes. She did not even glance around at the sound of Lynn's voice, and Lynn frowned as she went on to the next bed. Gwen was two beds away, and came across to her.

'I've been trying to get through to Ann,' said Gwen, 'but the night staff left a message to say that she was uncommunicative. Her mother died recently and her father has deserted her. She was being brought up by her grandmother, but the old lady isn't up to it so Ann has been rather neglected.'

'Poor child!' Lynn's sympathy was immediately aroused. 'What's wrong with her?'

'She's having her tonsils out, but she has been ill, too. I don't know if they will operate tomorrow. I think they're waiting to see how she fares today.'

Footsteps sounded and Lynn glanced around to see Paul and Sister Sloan making the morning round. Paul, seeing her, came along the ward after whispering to the Sister, who remained by the first bed, and Lynn steeled herself when she realised that he was coming to her. Gwen hastily moved away, and Lynn moistened her lips.

'Lynn,' said Paul in formal tones. 'Would you come over here for a moment, please?' He walked away from the beds and she followed. Then he glanced at the little newcomer in her bed, and lowered his tones. 'That's Ann Downey over there. No one seems to be able to communicate with her. She appears to have withdrawn into her own little world, and we don't like to operate while she's in that condition. You're the most capable nurse on the ward so I wonder if you would try to make a breakthrough. She hadn't been ill-treated, but she has been neglected, and the loss of her mother some time ago must have had a traumatic effect upon her.'

'Certainly.' Lynn nodded, her personal feelings forgotten. 'I was just learning some of the facts from Nurse Barber. I wondered why she didn't answer when I spoke to her. But she might be afraid, this being her first time in a hospital.'

'Well, try and get some animation in her, will you? I want her dealt with as quickly as possible so we can get her back on her feet again.'

'Is there anything you can tell me about her background? I know her mother is dead and her father deserted her. A grandmother was bringing, her up, but she's been neglected because her grandmother hasn't been well.'

'It's worse than that. The grand-mother is bedridden, and this child has been looking after her, until she became ill herself.'

'Doesn't she have any other family?'

'Not to our knowledge. The GP who asked for her admission says the grandmother is the only family he's found.'

'I'll see what I can do with her,' promised Lynn. 'Is she very ill now?'

'No. She's recovering from the illness, and, of course, her tonsils are to be removed. But I can't decide if she's in a fit state for the operation yet.' He paused, his features impassive. 'I won't see her on this round, but I'll come back to the ward later, after you've had the opportunity to work on her. If you get some response with your efforts, we'll go on from there.'

Lynn nodded and went back to Ann Downey's bedside, moving around to the far side so that she faced the child, who gazed ahead without showing reaction to Lynn's movement. Lynn crouched to peer into the still blue eyes, and she smiled slowly, calling upon all her experience to help.

'Hello, Ann,' she said softly. 'How are you feeling now? I hear that you've been very ill.'

There was no reply to her question, and no sign that the child had even heard the question.

'Have you seen all the other children in this ward, Ann?' she persevered. 'Some of them have been very, very ill, and we had to nurse them carefully to get them better. Is there anything I can do for you?' She paused, awaiting a reply, but none came, and she went on:

'Would you like a drink? Are you hungry?'

There was no reaction, and Lynn glanced at the little girl in the next bed.

'Jenny, have you spoken to Ann this morning?' she asked.

'Yes, Nurse, but she won't answer. I think she's deaf.'

Lynn shook her head. 'She's not deaf. She's just afraid and lonely. Are you missing your Nanny, Ann?'

The girl's eyes blinked, just once, then remained motionless, and Lynn was heartened, for it was the first reaction she had noted.

'Are you worried about your Nanny, Ann?' she probed. 'She's been ill, hasn't she? You've been taking care of her. You needn't worry, you know. She'll be taken care of while you're in here. We'll soon have you better and on your feet, then you'll be able to go back to your Nanny.'

'No!' The single syllable was uttered with great emphasis and, for a moment, the staring eyes glittered with inner fire.

Then all reaction drained away and the small face became composed again. Lynn caught her breath, a frown appearing between her brows.

'You don't want to go back to your Nanny?' she asked. 'Tell me about it, won't you? It helps, sometimes, if you can talk to someone, and I can listen. What's the trouble, Ann?'

The girl shook her head, and Lynn realised that she would get nothing more from her for the moment. She moved away from the bed, then went to Paul's side, and when she explained what she had learned, Paul nodded his satisfaction.

'Good,' he said. 'That's a great help. I had a feeling it was something like that. What we've got to do is get across to her that when she's better she won't be going back to the situation that existed before she was taken ill. The local authority won't permit her to be there alone with her Nanny. Do you think you could gain her confidence enough to accept that?'

'I'll try.' Lynn went back along the ward, and this time there was a flicker of interest in the child's eyes as she sat down on the side of the bed and reached out to take hold of a thin hand.

'I don't want to get better,' declared the girl fiercely.

'Why not? Tell me about it,' encouraged Lynn.

'Because I have to look after Nanny. I can't go out to play with my friends. I can't have anyone in to play.'

'You don't have to worry about that. The doctor tells me that when you are well, you won't be allowed to return to your Nanny's home under the conditions in which you lived. So just you try to get well as quickly as possible and then we'll see what happens, shall we?'

'Are you just telling me that?' There was suspicion glimmering in the pale eyes.

'No, Ann. I wouldn't tell fibs. Ask any of the children here. They'll all be your friends while you are with us, and you can trust all the nurses. The only reason why we're here is to help you.' Lynn glanced sideways as Paul walked past the bed without halting, and he was followed by Sister Sloan, who met Lynn's gaze and nodded her approval.

'I like my Nanny, but I don't like staying at her house.'

'We understand that, and it won't happen again. Now, tell me, are you hungry? Would you like something to drink?'

'Yes, please. I'm thirsty.'

Lynn smiled and patted the child's hand. 'I'll get you something,' she promised. 'Then we'll see how you feel. I do believe you're looking better already.'

She was rewarded with a shy smile, and as she left the bedside, a frown touched her face. She felt humble as she compared her own personal feelings, which she considered were overwhelmingly difficult to control, and the kind of situation a mere child had found herself to be in. She reported to Paul, and he nodded.

'Give her anything she wants. I'll see

her this afternoon. If she is all right, she can have the operation in the morning.'

Lynn went on with her work, and the time seemed to pass so quickly that she was surprised when Sister Sloan told her to go to lunch. She left the ward and went down to the dining-room. But Vince Braddock intercepted her before she could reach the sanctuary of its doors.

'I've been looking for an opportunity to see you all morning,' he said, when he confronted her. 'You didn't leave the Children's department once, did you?'

'No. We do work when we're on the wards,' she replied with a thin smile, and now her feelings were safely locked up behind a powerful barrier. 'I'm sorry if I spoiled your evening last night.'

'Think nothing of it. I didn't expect too much, and was thankful that I managed to get you at all. Perhaps I'll have better luck next time.'

'There won't be a next time, Vince.'

'Oh.' He grimaced. 'I have an uneasy

feeling that this time you really mean it.'

When Paul visited the ward later that afternoon, Lynn viewed him dispassionately, still gripped by a strange emotion which seemed to be purging her of ordinary attitudes. She could see that her own way of life during the past months had been self-centred and mediocre. She had actually considered herself to be ill-used because a romantic affair had turned out wrongly, and yet Ann Downey had come face to face with much harder facts of life, even at the tender age of eight.

'How is the child?' asked Paul, his face as expressionless as usual.

'She's coming along just fine,' responded Lynn. 'She's eaten her lunch and now she's talking to some of the other children. I promised her that she would not have to go back to the way she was living before she was taken ill, and I only hope that will be the case.'

'Don't worry. The local authorities

are handling the case now. The Nanny is being cared for in an old people's home, and young Ann will be taken into care. She'll be with children of her own age.'

'Good. She'll like that. I've been telling her what it would be like and she's quite happy with the idea.'

'Then you've done a good job with her.' There was commendation in his tone, and Lynn looked squarely into his face. He hesitated. 'Would you mind if I came out to your place this evening?' he asked.

'To do some riding?' she queried, and saw him nod. 'You are always welcome. My father extended an open invitation to you, didn't he?' She paused and nerved herself. 'I hope you won't bring Della out there with you, though. I see enough of her around the hospital.'

'Sparks always seem to fly when you two meet. I wonder why?'

'I often wonder about that myself,' she retorted. 'And I have my own pet theory about it. But that wouldn't interest you, Doctor. You can form your own opinion. You've been in my company off duty and also Della's so you are in a good position to judge.' She glanced around. 'Now I'd better get on with my work. I can see Sister Sloan watching me, and there is a rumour going the rounds that you and I are interested in one another, so the dear Sister may think that we are discussing matters which are not bound by duty. Isn't it ridiculous how these rumours become more absurd?' She smiled and left him.

That evening, Lynn felt disinclined towards human contact, and escaped from the house before her parents arrived. She sighed with relief when she reached the stables and began to saddle Goldy. She needed to get out into the open, in solitude, and consider her situation.

The evening was perfect, with sunlight streaming across the countryside. She saw small clumps of primroses along a hedgerow, and dismounted when she spotted the more shy violets, delicate in the undergrowth. She crouched and sniffed at the violets, closing her eyes and permitting the fragrant scent to intoxicate her senses.

Then the pounding of hoofs broke through her thoughts and she straightened up and glanced around at the approaching figure of Paul mounted on one of her father's horses. She suppressed a sigh as he reined in before her.

'Something wrong?' he demanded, eyeing her keenly. 'I saw you suddenly stop and dismount.'

'Nothing's wrong. I merely wanted to smell the violets. They are the first I've seen this year.'

'Shall I pick some for you?' he asked, dismounting.

'No, thank you.' Her tones were cold and distant, as she swung back into her saddle. 'Wild flowers would be out of place in a vase on top of the TV set, wouldn't they?'

'Sorry, I'm an idiot,' he retorted,

swinging back into his saddle. He pulled on the reins and turned the horse away. 'I'll stay over in that area,' he called over his shoulder. 'Then I won't interrupt your solitude.'

She opened her mouth to call him, but he was already galloping away, and she fought down the impulse to follow.

Riding on, she went to the end of the meadow and dismounted, leaning her arms upon the five-barred gate that separated her father's land from their neighbour's. She tried to analyse what her feelings would be if Paul did buy out Mrs. Wilkins. She certainly didn't want him as a neighbour if he married someone like Della, although she could not really see Della wanting to bury herself in the country.

She turned slowly to lean against the gate and around the meadows. Her father was appearing from the stables, and he rode towards Paul, who was at least a quarter of a mile away. She suppressed the urge to join them.

Sighing, she rode back to the stable, putting away the horse and entering the house to find her mother in the lounge.

'Hello, dear,' greeted Mrs. Avery. 'I thought you would have gone with your father and Paul.'

'I saw them, but I was already on my way in then. Where have they gone?'

'You know Paul mentioned to your father that he would like to buy a place around here, and Father said Mrs. Wilkins was thinking of selling and moving into town, so they've gone across to see if a sale can be effected.'

'Paul for a neighbour?'

Mrs. Avery glanced up quickly. 'I thought you and Paul were hitting it off very well together.'

'A lot of people have been thinking that, and I don't know where they got the idea from.' Lynn sat down and picked up a magazine, but she did not read it. Her eyes took in the words but they failed to register in her brain.

'You sound as if you're in a bad humour. That's unusual for you, Lynn.

Is something wrong?'

'No.' Lynn shook her head. 'Perhaps I'm letting work get on top of me a little, but it's nothing serious.'

'Paul was talking to us before he went out riding, and he seemed to think that you were in a mood over something. He felt that you suddenly changed towards him, although he says you've always spoken your mind.'

'He would say that! But what's wrong with that?'

'Nothing, dear! Are you falling in love with Paul?'

'What gives you that idea?'

'I can't think of any other reason why you should change so suddenly.' Mrs. Avery's eyes were narrowed and filled with speculation. 'You went out with Vince Braddock last night instead of accepting Paul.'

'Paul was out with Della Tate last night!' protested Lynn.

'Ah!' Mrs. Avery nodded. 'So that's it, is it?'

'What on earth are you talking about?'

161

Lynn tried to smile, but her face was stiff.

'You are in love with Paul. Don't try to deny it, Lynn because it shows in your face. So what's the problem? Why don't you set out to win him? Are you still hung up on Robert?'

'No, of course not! Paul doesn't want any romantic entanglements. That's what he said when he first came out here to ride.'

'A man can change his mind about things like that.'

'If he has changed his mind then he's picked Della, and it — it hurts to see her get him.'

'Jealousy will get you nowhere, Lynn. You won't attract him by acting the shrew.'

'I haven't done that, Mother. I wouldn't act that way. It's not me and you know it.'

'Listen, you've got nothing to lose by giving him some encouragement, Lynn. And I'll help you where I can.'

'Don't say anything to him, Mother.

162

I'd die if he guessed the truth.'

'You feel that being in love with someone is something to be ashamed of? If you do, then you are suffering from reaction to that affair with Robert. But I wouldn't say anything to Paul, rest assured. What I will do is invite him here for the week-end. That will throw the two of you together. He did say he's off duty this week-end. What about you? What shift are you doing next week?'

'Two till ten.' Lynn sighed heavily, but already there was a thin strand of hopeful optimism unwinding in her mind like a ball of brightly coloured wool. 'I finish for the week-end on Friday at five-thirty.'

'All right. Leave it to me. I'll get him here for the week-end, and you do your best to interest him.'

Lynn smiled and nodded. 'Oh, all right!' she said reluctantly. 'But I feel certain he'll snub me. He doesn't want anything to do with romance. That's why he asked me out in the first place, because he said he could rely on me to remain platonic.'

'You said you only asked him here to spite Della Tate, and yet here you are, in love with him!' Mrs. Avery smiled. 'I think we can sort this out, Lynn.'

'I'm going up to wash my hair. Then I'll go to bed.' Lynn went to the door. 'I won't come down again, Mother. Good night.'

'Good night, love, and keep your chin up. I think you have only to play your cards right to get what you want, so don't be foolish. Treat Paul like a man, and one who is important to you, and I think you'll find him eating out of your hand. You're used to handling horses, aren't you? Well, men are not much different when it comes to handling them.' Mrs. Avery smiled knowingly.

As Lynn left the house next day, she made a vow that she would do everything right today, and set off for the hospital in an eager frame of mind.

Upon arrival, she went to check on Ann Downey, and was relieved to find the child animated and friendly with her fellow patients.

'Hello, Nurse,' she said cheerfully. 'I'm going to have my operation today.'

'That's fine! You'll soon be better, Ann.'

'Doctor Morgan was talking to me. I told him that I've always wanted a pony of my own and he said you have a pony and a horse, and your father is a vet and has a lot of horses.'

'Have you ever ridden a pony?' inquired Lynn.

'No. I used to see one when my Dad took me out. But Dad has gone away and I don't know where he is. I'm going into a Home when I leave here.'

Lynn felt a tugging at her heart and she had to blink to repel the tears that threatened.

'You'll be happy there, with other children to play with, but I'll tell you what I'll do, Ann. When you're better and settled at the Home, I'll come and see you on my day off, and if you like I'll take you out to my home and let you ride my pony. He's getting old now, and I'm too heavy to ride him myself so he doesn't get all the exercise he needs.'

'Oh, Nurse!' There was incredulity in the child's tones, and her eyes shone. 'Would you really do that?'

'Of course. It's a promise!' Lynn smiled and patted the child's head. 'You've had nothing to eat or drink this morning, have you?'

'No. Doctor Morgan told me I shouldn't. What will the operation be like?'

'Don't worry yourself about it. You won't know anything. You will simply go to sleep, and when you wake up your tonsils will be gone. Just stay quiet on your bed and I'll come back to you shortly.'

She went along to the kitchen to start cleaning up, and was intent upon her work there when a footstep sounded in the doorway. Glancing around, expecting to see Sister Wade, she found Paul there, and he was smiling with delight.

'Lynn, I've just spoken to young Ann

166

Downey,' he said. 'She told me about your offer to let her ride your pony when she's better, and she's over the moon about it. We couldn't have found better medicine for her than that. Thank you for thinking of it.'

'The pony needs a young rider, and she expressed a liking for horses. She's going to be lonely and strange in a children's home when she leaves here so I thought I'd use some of my free time to see that she gets some individual attention.'

'Bless you, Lynn,' he said. 'You can flay the hide off anyone when you've a mind to, but it's not your true self, I know that.'

'It's good of you to say so,' she snapped, forgetting her good intentions, and he compressed his lips and backed away, lifting his hands as if to ward off her words.

'All right,' he placated. 'Take it easy. I seem to rub you up the wrong way every time I open my mouth.'

Sister Wade came to check up on her

a few minutes later, and found her leaning against the sink, a melancholy expression in her eyes.

'Come along, Nurse,' she snapped. 'There's a lot to be done this morning. Stop mooning over Doctor Morgan and let's get on with it.'

Lynn shook herself from her thoughts and went on with her work. By lunch-time, she had managed to, get her emotions under strict control, and before going off duty for an hour, she went along to the ward to find out how Ann Downey had fared. The girl had been operated on and was still unconscious, but there had been no complications, and Lynn went to lunch feeling relieved.

She was back on the wards within the hour, and found Ann Downey awake. The child was still hazy but smiled at sight of Lynn, who smoothed her hair and spoke gently to her. She attended to the wants of her other patients, and a sense of satisfaction filled her mind as she concentrated upon her work. Here she was needed, her skills an asset, and she forgot about Paul and her personal problems and was hard at it when Sister Wade returned.

'You'll be in Women's Medical next week on the afternoon shift,' said Sister Wade.

'Oh.' Lynn felt sharply disappointed. 'I was hoping I'd be kept on here, Sister. I've come to prefer working in Children's. You're not fed up with me, are you?'

'No. In fact, I saw the Assistant Matron and asked if I could keep you, and she's promised that after next week you'll be able to come back to me. They'll be short-staffed on Women's Medical next week and you're the most capable nurse we have.'

'That's a complete turn-round from the usual reports on me,' observed Lynn dryly.

'Haven't you heard that Nurse Tate is leaving the hospital?' asked Sister Wade.

'No.' Lynn frowned. 'I spoke to her this morning; tried to make friends with her. But she didn't want to know. Is this a sudden decision, Sister?'

'She saw Matron yesterday, it seems, and she's leaving at the end of the month.'

'The place won't be the same without her!' Lynn sighed, and wondered if Della's decision to leave had anything to do with Paul buying her neighbour's place. Surely Della hadn't hooked Paul to that extent!

'We discovered that she was responsible for most of the trouble for which you took the blame. I don't know whether Matron will have a few words with you, but it seems you've been badly maligned.'

Lynn smiled. 'Well, wonders never cease! I'd better get on with my work. If I have a brand-new reputation now, I don't want it tarnished in any way. Thank you for the news, Sister.'

She hummed to herself as she continued through the afternoon, and it seemed that there was only one black spot in her whole life. Paul Morgan! He walked into the ward just before five to check up on the post-operatives, and she suppressed an emotional sigh as she studied his tall figure. He seemed farther from her now than at any time in the last few years.

Friday passed inevitably, and Lynn discovered that word of Della Tate's intention to leave the staff brought a spate of rumours about their colleague's future, some of them very wild.

Lynn found herself being congratulated by nurses who had recently almost ignored her, and she found her hours easier to bear as a consequence. When she was getting ready to go off duty, she went along to Ann Downey's bed. The girl was sitting up and looking fine.

'I'm going off duty for the week-end, Ann,' Lynn said, glancing around. 'Normally you would be out of here before the week-end, but as you've been ill, they're keeping you for a few more days. When you are better, I'll see about having you come to my home. You would like that, wouldn't you?'

'Oh, yes, please! I can't think of anything else since you told me. You won't change your mind, will you, Nurse?'

'Don't worry about that,' Lynn reassured her. 'I wish you were well enough to come home with me now. But there will be other times soon, and I'll keep in touch with you.'

'Oh, thank you, Nurse.' The child hugged Lynn round the neck.

Quite touched, Lynn went to the car park. As she was getting into her car, she saw Paul emerging from the main entrance, with Della at his side. They both got into Paul's car and he drove away, glancing sideways at Lynn as he passed her car. He seemed to look coolly in her direction, and she sat with pinched lips, refusing to meet Della's gaze, for fear that the girl would be wearing her usual smug smile.

She was thoughtful as she drove

homeward and after tea went out to the stables. She rode out across the meadow, wanting to be alone, and it was about two hours later when she saw her father riding towards her, waving as he came.

'Hello, Father!' she greeted him when he reined in beside her. 'Taking the evening off?'

'I am entitled to one now and again,' he responded. 'How are you getting along?'

'Fine. Everything is working out well. I've been under a cloud at the hospital for some time, but it has begun to lift.' She paused as her father glanced around. 'I saw you riding across to Mrs. Wilkins's place. Is Paul thinking of buying?'

'More than just thinking, my dear. He made an offer and Mrs. Wilkins accepted on the strength of my recommendation of Paul's suitability as a neighbour. Your mother and I have great hopes now. You know that I did entertain ideas about buying that property should it come on the market, and indeed Mrs. Wilkins did promise me the chance of first refusal. But I've been thinking lately that you and Paul might get together and the place would be in the family then. That's why I pushed Paul into considering making the purchase.'

'Perhaps you shouldn't have jumped to conclusions, Father. Paul comes here to ride your horses, but he's also seeing another nurse in his spare time. That's his business, of course,' she added.

'But I thought — !' He broke off and shook his head. 'Now I don't know what to think. Anyway, it's none of my business. I just hope you won't get hurt again, Lynn.'

'I'm not likely to,' she retorted with a smile.

'Is Paul coming this evening?'

'I don't know. He didn't say anything when I saw him this afternoon.'

'He's a good rider, and he has made plans for the future. I could tell that. But I'll be disappointed if the bride he installs next door isn't you.'

'I've never shown the slightest interest in him, so I don't know why you and Mother should jump to conclusions about us. Unless it was wishful thinking.'

'No, it wasn't that. It seemed that the pair of you were ideally suited.'

'Well, most marriages are made in heaven, so they say.' Lynn smiled wryly. 'But a great many of them get broken on Earth or fail to mature. I wonder how many true lovers have failed to meet up with their intended and had to make do with second best!'

'Let's take a ride,' her father suggested. 'If I didn't know you better, I would think you were becoming morbid.'

Lynn made no reply, but accompanied him dutifully, although she would have preferred to have been alone. But she kept glancing around, hoping to see Paul appear on one of the horses and when a rider did emerge from the stable, her pulses seemed to race, until she recognised her mother's slight figure. Her father excused himself and went galloping off towards the distant figure.

Lynn rode back to the stable by a roundabout way to avoid talking to her mother. She did not want to have to answer any awkward questions, and after taking care of her horse, she went into the house and sat in the lounge. Paul would not come now, she thought, as she recalled him driving away from the hospital with Della at his side. He would be in Della's company this evening, no doubt.

Lynn viewed the week-end with unenthusiastic consideration. She could almost hope that Monday would come forward to oust Saturday and Sunday so that she could get back to work and lose herself in duty. But time was an implacable enemy and she knew it would have to be faced, hour by lonely hour.

Eventually, Lynn's restlessness drove her out of the house and she motored into the town centre, passing the hospital and glancing at the vehicles in the car park in the yard. Paul's car was not there, and she deduced he was not on duty. She went to the multi-storey park and left her car there, then walked towards the little pub, where she was immediately button-holed by Vince, who seemed to have made an early start on some serious drinking. He staggered slightly as he grasped her arm, and led her to a side table despite the calls of some of the nurses at the big table by the window.

'I thought you weren't coming in here again,' remarked Vince, peering rather owlishly at her. 'Are you looking for Paul and Della? They were here together earlier, but didn't stay.'

'I came because I felt lonely,' she replied. 'But if you're going to talk about Paul and Della, then I'll go back home.'

'No, don't do that. Make my life tolerable, Lynn, and stay with me. What would you like to drink?'

'Nothing alcoholic, thank you,' she said firmly, and when he went to the bar, she arose and crossed to the table where her friends were seated, greeting them cheerfully. But there was a worried frown on Chrissie's face, and Lynn sat down beside her friend.

'Lynn, I'm so glad you've come in,' said the girl. 'Vince is on call this evening, but he's drinking far too much. If there is an emergency, he won't be fit to take it!'

'I thought he was off duty!' A frown creased Lynn's forehead as she turned and looked at Vince, who was making his way un-steadily steadily back to his table, motioning for her to rejoin him. 'What's set him on this bender, do you know?'

'You, of course,' said Chrissie anxiously. 'You must know how he feels about you.'

'I know, but I can't help that. I'd better go and try to talk some sense into him. See you later.' She rose and went back to Vince's table, thanking him for the soft drink he had bought her, but eyeing him with stern disapproval. 'I thought you were off duty,' she said firmly. 'What are you doing drinking, Vince?'

'A man has to forget sometimes,' he retorted. 'I've had about as much as I can take. I've reached the crossroads, Lynn, and I've got to make up my mind which way I'm going in future.'

'You're talking about me, of course,' she said softly. 'I'm sorry, Vince.'

'Not as sorry as I am. I think I'm going to have to leave the hospital and try to make a fresh start somewhere else, Lynn.'

'Because of me!' She stifled a sigh. 'If you can't forget about me, then it seems to be the only course left open to you, Vince.'

'You're stuck on Morgan, I know that! How are you going to live with that? Della's got her hooks into him. I didn't think she'd manage it after you had him out to your home, but she's got around him.'

'I heard that Della is leaving us.' Lynn spoke huskily. 'So she won't be around much longer.'

'She's leaving nursing altogether! But she won't be leaving the town. She'll still be seeing Morgan, until she tires of him. You know what she's like.'

'So let's discuss you and forget about Della and Paul,' said Lynn. 'You've had more than enough to drink, Vince. If you should be called out to an emergency, you won't be able to cope.'

'I haven't had that much to drink!' he protested, lifting a tall glass of beer and draining it at a gulp. 'Who cares, anyway?'

'I care about your future,' she retorted. 'You've worked too hard in the past to throw everything away like this. You're behaving like a schoolboy instead of a grown man. This situation is something you have to face up to. You can't run away from it.'

'Like you faced up to losing Robert?' He smiled at her, his lips stiff.

'I did face up to it, and I got over it,'

she countered. 'It wasn't easy, but I beat it, and you can do the same.'

'Well, I don't think I shall be called out,' he snapped. 'If you don't like to see me drink, then go back to your friends over there. They find me a figure of ridicule because of you. But I don't care what they think.' He arose and went to the bar to refill his glass, and Lynn felt a pang of alarm as she saw that he was very unsteady indeed. She went back to Chrissie's table.

'I can't stop him drinking,' she reported, 'and if there is an emergency, he won't be in any fit state to handle it. If he so much as walks into the hospital in that state, he'll be in trouble.'

'There's nothing we can do about it,' stated Chrissie. 'He's old enough to know what he's doing, Lynn.'

'Perhaps, but I know how he feels, if you don't. I wonder where Paul went this evening? Is he out with Della, do you know?'

'She left the hospital with him when

we went off duty,' said Chrissie.

'I know. I saw them together. I wonder what his telephone number is?' Lynn rose and went to the door. There was a public telephone box just outside, and she entered and looked through the directory, finding Paul's address and number. She called the number, and was about to hang up because there was no reply, when she heard a response from the other end of the line. It was Della Tate's voice.

Lynn froze at the sound and, for a moment, the world seemed to totter. What was Della doing at Paul's flat, and why had it taken someone so long to answer? She drew a long, shuddering breath and moistened her lips.

'I'd like to speak to Paul, please, Della,' she said evenly.

'Lynn?' A note of surprise edged Della's voice. There was a short pause. 'Just a moment, I'll fetch him.'

Lynn waited, her mind seemingly paralysed. Then Paul's voice sounded in her ear.

'What's the matter, Lynn?' He sounded impatient, and Lynn compressed her lips, then explained the situation tersely. When she lapsed into silence, he cleared his throat, then spoke slowly. 'Well, he's a darned fool, that's all I can say. Surely you don't expect me to come down there and either sober him up or take his place, do you? He's been trying to get at me over you for a long time.'

'This isn't the time for personalities to clash,' Lynn insisted. 'I know Vince will get into trouble if he's called and they find he's the worse for drink! But I'm thinking of the patients who might need expert attention, and I think you should do the same.'

'All right.' Paul's voice was crisp. 'I'll be at the pub in ten minutes. Keep him there, and if anyone comes for him, tell them I'll be handling any emergency.'

'Thank you, and I'm sorry to spoil your evening,' Lynn retorted. She hung up and left the telephone box, her eyes moist with unshed tears, her mind filled with conjecture. Vince thought he had problems, but she knew that she was equally at a loss.

'Where have you been?' Vince demanded when she got back. 'I thought you'd run out on me again.'

'I've been arranging for you to be covered should there be an emergency,' she answered. 'You're in no fit state to be on call-out.'

'I don't need you to arrange anything for me,' he snapped. 'I can take care of myself.'

'It's not you I'm thinking of,' she said. 'It's the patients.'

That silenced him and he sat moodily, gazing around the room. Lynn was tense, keeping an eye on the door for the first sign of Paul, and when he entered the lounge and paused in the doorway, she lifted a hand to attract his attention.

'What the devil is he doing here?' demanded Vince, catching sight of Paul as he approached their table.

'I sent for him!' Lynn's voice was unemotional.

Paul came and sat down opposite Lynn, beside Vince, and he needed no more than a glance to judge Vince's condition.

'I'll take over duty from you, Braddock,' he stated in crisp tones. 'You're not fit to answer any calls.'

'It's my duty and I'll do it,' retorted Vince. 'Who needs your help?'

'You'll do as you're told, and if you have any sense at all, you'll stop making a fool of yourself,' Paul said.

'That's what I've been telling him,' cut in Lynn. 'Hadn't you better inform the hospital that you're taking over, Paul?'

He glanced at her, nodding grimly. 'I've already done that, so I'll have to go back home as quickly as possible in case there's a call-out.'

Lynn thought of Della waiting back there for him, and clenched her teeth. She nodded.

'I'm sorry I have to call you out, but I

couldn't think of any other way to resolve this particular problem. You don't really mind, do you?'

'No.' He shook his head. 'I know what Braddock is feeling like. He has my sympathies. But he should face up to it like a man. I'll walk you to your car, if you like. It's in the multi-storey car park, I assume.'

'It is, but I'll be all right. I'm not afraid to go there alone.'

'Then you should be, from all the accounts that I've heard about it.' Paul rose and stood gazing down at Vince, who was slumped in his seat. 'I'll be handling your duties until tomorrow morning, Braddock,' he observed. 'You'd better be ready to take over at nine. I'm not going to be available after then. Have you got that?'

Vince lifted his head and looked up at Paul, then tried to focus his gaze upon Lynn, but his head lolled sideways and he smiled sheepishly.

'I'll be all right in the morning,' he said. 'I'll be all right.'

Lynn turned and walked to the door, followed by Paul, and she paused to turn and smile and wave good-bye to her friends. She saw an expression of concern on Chrissie's face, but widened her smile and departed.

Out in the street, she faced Paul with a trace of defiance in her eyes. 'Look, it's all right, thank you, but I can manage by myself. I've already put you to a lot of trouble this evening, and spoiled your off-duty time.'

'Nonsense! You did the right thing. The duty must be covered at the hospital. Now say no more and I'll walk you to your car. I don't want any arguments, thank you. Just do as you're told for once.'

Lynn fell silent, feeling like a schoolgirl who had been reprimanded in front of an entire class. They walked to the car park, and she pointed to Vince's car.

'I'm afraid that he may try to drive home later, Paul,' she said warily.

'I'll go back to the pub and sort him

out,' he retorted. 'Just get into your car and go, Lynn, and in future don't trifle with the emotions of your colleagues.'

'That's unfair!' Her cheeks burned and an angry glitter appeared in her eyes. 'I've never encouraged Vince. In fact, I've always pointed out to him exactly how I feel about him.'

'You finally gave in and let him take you out for an evening.'

'But I said it didn't mean anything and he acknowledged that fact.'

'Perhaps he did, but he was encouraged, and now look at him. I won't be around to stand in for him tomorrow, and if he's unable to do his duty, he'll be in trouble.'

'All right, I'm going!' Lynn fumbled in her handbag for her car keys, and opened the door. He moved aside for her, his face set in harsh lines, and as she drove away she glanced in her rearview mirror and saw his tall figure motionless, his face in deep shadow as he watched her departure.

6

Because she had such a poor night's sleep, Lynn did not awaken until fairly late, and for a moment she was concerned that she might have over-slept and made herself late for duty. Then she remembered that it was Saturday and the week-end was upon her, stretching away into the future like an emotional obstacle.

She could not hear any sounds in the house and realised that her parents would already have left to go about their business. She arose slowly and showered, then dressed in jeans and a sweater. She was thoughtful as she went down to breakfast, and it was in her mind that she would just laze around for the entire week-end. She greeted Mrs. Moss when she entered the kitchen, and the housekeeper smiled as she made a pot of tea.

'I heard you moving around up there and knew you'd soon be coming down,' said Mrs. Moss. 'Did you sleep well, Lynn?'

'I'm afraid not! Now I don't feel like doing anything.'

'Well you're off duty until Monday, so you can please yourself how you spend your time. You need a complete rest now and again, Lynn. But have you forgotten that Doctor Morgan is coming here for the week-end?'

'He isn't!'

'When did he tell you that?'

'He didn't.' Lynn tossed her head. 'He would have said something last night if he were coming.'

'Your mother told me this morning before she left with your father that he would be here at nine-thirty or thereabouts, and that he would be staying in the house over the week-end.'

'What?' Lynn glanced at the kitchen clock on the wall. The time was nine-twenty, and she knew Paul was punctual if nothing else. 'But why didn't someone say something to me yesterday?'

'I gathered from what was said that you knew about the arrangements several days ago,' said Mrs. Moss, smiling. 'But that's nothing to get upset about. Sit you down and I'll give you some breakfast. If you think you're going to have an easy week-end then you'll have to think again, because the doctor is coming to do some work on the stable. No doubt he'll expect you to help him. I think that was your mother's idea, to have the two of you together here alone.'

'Well, it isn't a good idea, and if he shows up I won't see him.'

'I think I can hear a car outside now,' retorted the housekeeper, putting a bowl of cereal in front of Lynn. 'You sit there and eat your breakfast while I'll go and attend to your guest.'

'He's not my guest,' retorted Lynn angrily, but Mrs. Moss smiled and departed quickly to the front of the house.

Lynn realised that she was acting like a spoiled child, and ate her breakfast determinedly, narrowing her blue eyes when she heard voices in the hall. But there was an ache in her breast and she steeled herself for what would be a bitter-sweet ordeal. She wanted to see Paul, and yet the sight of him would upset her peace of mind.

He opened the door for Mrs. Moss and followed the housekeeper into the kitchen, closing the door gently and turning to smile cheerfully at Lynn.

'Good morning,' he said brightly. 'Sorry to arrive so early. I wouldn't have come had I known you were going to lie in.'

'I didn't know you were coming at all until Mrs. Moss told me about it five minutes ago,' replied Lynn. 'Would you like some tea? I assume that you've had breakfast.'

'Thank you.' He nodded and pulled out a chair opposite her, seating himself and smiling at Mrs. Moss. 'I've had breakfast, thanks, but a cup of tea would do fine.'

'About last night,' began Lynn, but he held up a hand and, for a moment, his face held a serious expression.

'Let's forget about last night, shall we?' he suggested.

She sighed and nodded slowly. 'It would probably be the best thing to do,' she agreed, resuming her breakfast. 'What about Vince though? Will he be on duty today?'

'I've already checked with the hospital. He's called in and reported that he's on stand-by.'

'I'm glad to hear that. But I really didn't expect you to be here for the week-end.'

'Shall I be in your way?' His eyes bored into hers, and Lynn forced a smile as she shook her head.

'I don't think so. What is this job you're going to do around here?'

'There's a leak in the stable roof. I told your father I'd fix it. When I'm off duty for the week-end, the time drags with nothing in particular to do, so I'll be helping around here and you can see to it that I don't feel lonely.'

She almost mentioned Della, but bit her bottom lip. 'I'm not going to be around,' she replied, shaking her head. 'I'm going to turn out my bedroom and give it a spring-clean.'

'Oh, no, you're not!' snorted Mrs. Moss. 'That's my job, and I'll have you know that your room was thoroughly turned out only this week — three days ago, to be exact.'

'Oh.' Lynn was taken aback and looked at Paul with frowning gaze. 'If you're going up on to the roof then be careful. It isn't too safe. You could fall through.'

'Is it as bad as all that?' He shook his head. 'Well, I'll examine it before I put my weight upon it. Only a fool would rush in where an angel would fear to tread, you know.'

'Are you inferring that I always rush in when I ought not to?' she demanded.

'If the cap fits,' he remarked,

chuckling. 'Are you going riding today?'

'I expect so. But I'll stick around the yard to watch you just in case you fall off the stable roof.'

'Thanks. You're well up in first aid, aren't you?'

The ghost of a smile touched her lips and she arose from the table. 'Thank you, Mrs. Moss,' she said, and walked to the door, glancing back at Paul as she did so. 'I see you're dressed for the part of a labourer, so why not set to work? If you'll come this way, I'll show you where the ladder is.'

Lynn turned and left the kitchen, pausing on the step to glance around. The day was fine, the sun warm, and she felt her spirits rise as she took stock. Paul was here for the whole week-end. Could she not just accept that fact and enjoy every moment of it?

Thus, when she turned to face him as he emerged from the kitchen, there was a smile on her face.

'Hello!' he exclaimed, his keen eyes

upon her face. 'You've changed expression. That means you're up to something, if I know anything about you. What have you done? Probably half-sawn through the rungs of the ladder, I'll wager!'

Lynn suppressed a sign, aware that he was not being malicious because there was a tight smile upon his lips.

'If you want my help today, then you'll have to be nice to me,' she told him, and turned to walk to the stables, leaving him staring after her in surprise.

They reached the stable and Lynn studied him curiously as he fetched out the ladder. She wondered exactly what was passing through his mind. Why had he made an effort to come into her life, stating that he wanted no emotional entanglements, then turned to Della? He knew of the animosity that existed between her and Della, that his conduct would obviously affect their relationship.

'I'll take a look from inside first,' he said, interrupting her thoughts. 'Show me exactly where the leak is. I suspect that the tiles are loose, and probably need cementing. Your father says there's a bag of ready-mixed cement in the garage. He bought it specially to do this job but couldn't find the time to get around to it.'

'Now where does the water come in?' he asked.

Lynn showed him, pointing to an area of the sloping roof. He nodded at once.

'Yes. Look there! You can see daylight coming through. A couple of tiles have been dislodged. But the roof doesn't look as if it is safe to stand on so I'd better put a board on it to spread my weight. If I work from the right, I'll be on that rafter there.'

'I don't weigh as much as you,' she said hesitantly. 'If you mix the cement, I'll go up there and put the tiles in place.'

'What about your lily-white hands?' He grinned.

'Now who's being nasty? You could

take a leaf out of your own book, you know. Perhaps you don't realise it, but you have such a superior manner.'

At her words, he studied her for a moment, then moistened his lips. 'Look, if my presence here irritates you in any way, then I'll do this job as I promised your father and leave.'

'What gives you the impression that I dislike your presence?'

'Your manner. You don't speak to Braddock in that tone. In the pub the other evening, you were acting quite normally towards him, and there was no sting in your tone. But whenever you speak to me, you sound positively waspish.' He sighed. 'You've got me thinking that you hate the sight of me. I know you only agreed to go out with me on that first evening because you wanted to spite Della, but am I really so objectionable to you?'

'Well!' She set her jaw firmly. 'You only asked me because Vince was bragging about taking me out. We started even, didn't we? You didn't want any emotional entanglements, and you haven't got them from me.'

'You also wanted nothing to do with romance, and you must know that your manner is calculated to kill any thoughts of romance in even the most determined man.'

'Yet you turned round and went out with Della,' she accused.

'You went out with Vince, knowing that he has always been in love with you.'

'He knows what the situation is between us,' she commented. 'Come on, I'll fetch a pail of water while you put up the ladder.'

Lynn fetched a pail and filled it with water. When she returned to the stable, Paul had the ladder propped up against the wall and was standing on the upper rungs, his head and shoulders above the edge of the roof. He was struggling to get a heavy plank into position on the red tiles.

'Anything I can do to help?' she called.

'Yes. Stand by to catch me if I should fall,' he retorted.

'Be careful!' Anxiety sounded plainly in her tones, and he paused and glanced down at her.

'Nurse, if I fell off here, you'd calmly check that I was still alive, then go for a ride on Goldy.'

Lynn fought down the sharp retort she instinctively began to make, although it proved to be an effort. 'Poor Della would be upset if they took you into Casualty today. She's on duty there.'

'I know. She told me so last night,' he said sharply.

Lynn clenched her teeth, struggling against a pang of jealousy. He finished putting the plank into position, then climbed on to it.

'Be careful,' she called. 'I can hear the timbers creaking.'

'My weight is spread along the length of the plank,' he assured her, vanishing from her sight. 'You may not know it, but I am quite a good do-it-yourself man. I'm not just a pretty face.'

'You're not even a pretty face!' she joked, and he chuckled.

Then she heard an urgent shout from Paul.

'Look out. Stand clear!'

She sprang backwards as she heard a grating sound, and the next instant a tile came sliding off the roof and crashed to the ground at her feet. If she hadn't moved, it would have struck her. She heard Paul's muttered imprecation, and then he was descending rapidly from the roof, almost hurling himself down the ladder.

'Lynn, are you all right?' he cried anxiously. Before she could answer, she saw the ladder slip to the right, and hurried forward to grasp it, preventing its movement. At that precise moment, Paul's right shoe came off and fell upon her upturned face. The heel struck her bottom lip, and she tasted the saltiness of blood as she averted her head.

'I'm sorry, Lynn. Here, let me look.'

He took her face between his hands

and held her despite her struggles.

'I'm all right. For heaven's sake, put on your shoe and let's get this job done. I want to go riding today, not tomorrow.'

'You're going to have a bruise there, I'm afraid, and the corner of your mouth is split.'

'I'll tell my father that you hit me,' she snapped.

'That would please him. He told me that's probably what you needed.'

'What?' She stared at him, struck speechless.

'That's right. He told me the other evening that if I wanted to tame you, I might have to use a bit of force — like one would take a riding crop to a fractious horse.'

'Why on earth would my father think that you should want to tame me?' she cried. 'Anyway, who says I need taming?'

'Oh, you need it, darling!' he said, smiling, and despite her struggles she could not get away from him. His left hand slid around to the back of her neck and he held her firmly but gently. He reached into his pocket and produced a handkerchief, gently dabbing at her bleeding lip. 'But then again, perhaps all you need is for someone to show you some love and understanding. I can see that my impossible, stand-offish attitude isn't working, because relations between us have deteriorated drastically since that first evening.'

Lynn could only gaze up into his piercing brown eyes, finally at a loss for words. The next moment, he bent his head and kissed her lightly on the mouth, being very careful to avoid her bruised lip.

Then something exploded in Lynn's mind, and she pushed him away fiercely, her eyes glittering, her shoulders heaving as he left her breathless.

'What do you think you're doing?' she demanded. 'Haven't you done enough already, without adding to it?'

He frowned, his eyes boring into

hers. 'What do you mean?'

'You push yourself into my life, telling me before we went out together that you wanted nothing to do with any woman. All you wanted was company. You didn't want to get involved.'

'So?' His tones were suddenly low pitched and careful.

'So I fell in love with you. I was in love with you before this business of seeing each other began, although I didn't realise it. But after that first night you came riding here, I knew I was in love with you, and I had to be hateful towards you to cover the fact.'

'You're in love with me?' There was a soft wonder in his voice.

'That's what I said,' she rapped angrily.

'Just a moment.' His hands were upon her shoulders. 'You're still biting my head off. Would you please try to say you love me as if you meant it?'

'Why should I? I've been fighting against it ever since I discovered the fact.'

'You see! That's what I mean. You don't want anything to do with love. You have had one love affair that turned out in an unfortunate way and you're afraid to gamble upon another.'

'It's you who didn't want to get involved. I keep telling you that I deliberately fought down my feelings because you said you didn't want to become involved.'

'We're talking at cross purposes!' His voice was low, almost a caress. 'I love you, Lynn. I've loved you for as long as I can remember.'

'Then what about Della? You knew she and I never got along, but you flaunted her in my face, knowing that she had boasted to the nurses that she would be the first to hook you.'

'I'm afraid you do poor Della a great injustice!' Paul smiled as he spoke. 'She wanted something from me and I made a deal with her. She was to see me off duty if I gave her what she wanted. She agreed, and the ploy worked. You became jealous and now you've admitted that you are in love with me.'

'What did Della want from you?' Lynn demanded suspiciously.

He chuckled. 'You thought she was after me,' he retorted. 'Well, she was playing a much bigger fish than an ordinary hospital practitioner. She's leaving the hospital to marry a man who is practically a millionaire, and he's buying a mansion for her and having it fitted out as a nursing home. She wanted advice from me on how to set about establishing it, and I agreed to help her in that respect if she helped me get to you.'

'But she was at your flat last night.'

'So was her fiancé, but you didn't hear his voice on the phone, did you?'

Lynn's mind was in a whirl. Her lip was beginning to throb painfully, but despite that, a wild excitement and certainty was growing in her heart. She looked up into Paul's smiling face, and suddenly all the barriers vanished and the bitterness of the past was gone, washed away by the rising tide of love which flooded through her.

'Paul, after the way I treated you, would you still do me a favour?'

'Of course, sweetheart,' he said huskily.

'Kiss me again, then tell me you love me in a tone which will sound as if you meant it.'

'I will if you promise to do the same,' he countered.

'I love you, Paul!' She spoke in a whisper, and tears of happiness filtered into her eyes. 'How stupid I've been!'

'And I love you, Lynn!' His voice was vibrant with emotion, and he took her gently into his arms and kissed her. 'My dear, impetuous nurse! I love you with all my heart.'

We do hope that you have enjoyed reading this large print book.

Did you know that all of our titles are available for purchase?

We publish a wide range of high quality large print books including:
Romances, Mysteries, Classics
General Fiction
Non Fiction and Westerns

Special interest titles available in large print are:
The Little Oxford Dictionary
Music Book, Song Book
Hymn Book, Service Book

Also available from us courtesy of Oxford University Press:
Young Readers' Dictionary
(large print edition)
Young Readers' Thesaurus
(large print edition)

For further information or a free brochure, please contact us at:
Ulverscroft Large Print Books Ltd.,
The Green, Bradgate Road, Anstey,
Leicester, LE7 7FU, England.
Tel: (00 44) **0116 236 4325**
Fax: (00 44) **0116 234 0205**

A MOST UNUSUAL CHRISTMAS

Fenella J. Miller

Cressida Hadley is delighted when Lord Bromley and his family are unexpectedly obliged to spend Christmas at her family home, the Abbey. True, Bromley's brother has a broken leg, her father and the earl have taken an instant dislike to each other, and the Dowager Lady Bromley drinks too much — but Cressida is convinced she can overcome these difficulties to arrange a merry holiday season. However, she has not taken into consideration the possibility that she might fall in love with Lord Bromley himself . . .

Laois

WHERE WE BELONG

Angela Britnell

Blamed for his sister's tragic death, estranged from his family, and his career in tatters, American Broadway singing star Liam Delaroche travels to Trelanow in Cornwall, searching for a new life. Meanwhile, local schoolteacher Ellie Teague is on a mission to establish her independence after jilting Will, her longtime fiancé. The attraction between the two is instant and electric. But the shadow of Liam's past looms over their growing relationship — and then the first of his bitter family members shows up in Trelanow . . .